THIS ...
POSSIBL...

She was much too ...
to have come from ...
were allowed in the hotel. The manager had been
adamant about it, in fact. I thought for a moment.
There was no choice. I had to go and find out.

I threw on a bathrobe, told the cat to stay put, and
took the elevator down to the room directly beneath
mine. I was so confused and excited that I didn't realize the inappropriateness of knocking on someone's
hotel door at two in the morning.

I needn't have worried. The door was opened immediately after I'd knocked. Standing there in a pair of
very expensive silk pajamas was a shortish woman in
her forties. Around her neck was a woolen muffler,
and on her feet were big, puffy ski boots.

I didn't understand the queer way she was dresssed.
And I didn't understand why the front of her pajamas
was stained in blood. . . .

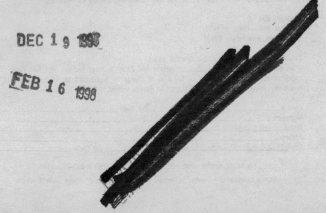

A CAT ON A WINNING STREAK

An Alice Nestleton Mystery

Lydia Adamson

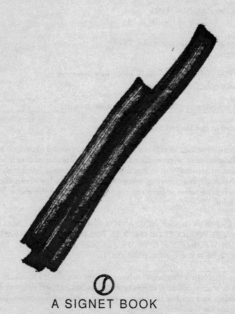

A SIGNET BOOK

SIGNET
Published by the Penguin Group
Penguin Books USA Inc., 375 Hudson Street,
New York, New York 10014, U.S.A.
Penguin Books Ltd, 27 Wrights Lane,
London W8 5TZ, England
Penguin Books Australia Ltd, Ringwood,
Victoria, Australia
Penguin Books Canada Ltd, 10 Alcorn Avenue,
Toronto, Ontario, Canada M4V 3B2
Penguin Books (N.Z.) Ltd, 182–190 Wairau Road,
Auckland 10, New Zealand

Penguin Books Ltd, Registered Offices:
Harmondsworth, Middlesex, England

First published by Signet, an imprint of Dutton Signet,
a division of Penguin Books USA Inc.

First Printing, May, 1995
10 9 8 7 6 5 4 3 2 1

Copyright © Lydia Adamson, 1995
All rights reserved

The first chapter of this book previously appeared in
A Cat on the Cutting Edge

 REGISTERED TRADEMARK—MARCA REGISTRADA

Printed in the United States of America

Chapter 1

It would soon be Valentine's Day. Only six more days. I couldn't wait.

No, that spurious holiday was hardly one of the high points of my year—not usually. I wasn't the little pigtailed blonde all the second grade farmboys gifted with construction paper hearts and penny candies. Valentine's Day arrived in the middle of February, usually a gray and soul-taxing month in New York City, let alone in Minnesota, where I was born. It has been many more years than I care to recall since a man brought me flowers and called me his valentine. *And,* truth be told, I suffer an actual, visceral disgust at this particular holiday, and have since that long-ago February 14 when my ex-husband and I had the row that ended with me falling on the ice in Rockefeller Center and breaking my front tooth.

So what made that upcoming St. Valentine's Day unlike any other? I had a job, that's what.

And I was being driven to it—chauffeured to it—in the backseat of one of those grotesque stretch limousines. Picked up at my own doorstep in Manhattan and driven via the Garden State Parkway . . . to Atlantic City.

I wasn't going to Atlantic City to bet on anything. I'm no gambler. And I wasn't going to catch Wayne Newton or Engelbert Humperdink either. I was going there to work. I actually had an acting job . . . in Atlantic City.

The marketing manager of a casino-hotel called Monte Carlo, on the famous boardwalk, had conceived a most unusual Valentine's Day promotion to lure people to his hotel and its gaming tables. The Monte Carlo was putting on a special Valentine's Day extravaganza for lovers who also love the theater. The show was to star a revered and famous actor and an actress whose stature was almost as elevated—in fact, they are husband and wife—in the great love scenes from the world of theater.

Directing the show would be a genuinely talented man—some called him a genius—whose future had once seemed as bright as any star in the heavens—New York, London, Hollywood all at his feet. But his flame had drowned very quickly, at the bottom of the bottle. And so, for years, he made a respectable living and had a fairly respectable career, instead of a stellar one. He directed projects such as the one we were involved in like falling off a log. Until signing on for this particular one, that is. The director dropped dead ten days ago.

There were a few other problems with the production. Chiefly, both leading man and leading lady had backed out when they realized that the casino's first salary offer was also its best and last salary offer. The famous couple could not see their way to accepting wages like that even in the service of a cause such as great theater or continuing education, which was one of their pet charities.

So the Monte Carlo was settling for less in every way. Their first big compromise was me, I suppose. I was offered the leading lady part, and took it, after I-don't-know-who-or-how-many-others turned it down. *Great Lovers Onstage* could just as well have been regarded as a brilliant promotional scheme as the supremely dumb idea I felt it to be. But I don't get paid for telling the people who hire me how to spend their money. Maybe the casino thought it was New Jersey's answer to Monaco. So what? That didn't bother me. If that's what they wanted, I'd play excerpts of every woman in love from Clytemnestra to Nellie Forbush.

The leading man, Gordon Seaver, was not such a big disappointment to the star-conscious people at the casino, I'm sure. Gordon Seaver had risen to stardom in the late 1950s as the strong back, long jaw, aw shucks, sweet-talking, song-belting tenor in half the legendary musical comedies on Broadway. He had, as they say, worked with them all. He'd even made it into two or three of the movie versions.

As for the new director, one Carlos Weathers, he was about to be famous, the word was. He was on the way up as quickly as the late-departed genius had been on the way down. Presumably, there would be a limo waiting for him when his plane landed later in the evening. Mr. Weathers was coming to us fresh from some triumph at a garage theater on the North Side of Chicago.

The monstrosity Gordon Seaver and I were riding in had all kinds of amenities, including a bar, a television set, a small sink, several plush designer towels, and the very latest, very glossiest foreign fashion magazines, to name just a few.

Gordon, after he introduced himself to me in Manhattan, had not said a word since, except for one brief and bitter monologue on how he despised winter. He was a handsome, large man with a full head of wavy brown-gray hair and an archetypal "good" profile, if not a very interesting one.

You would think that two old troupers like us would have a lot to talk about, but it simply wasn't so. Strangers through and through. The only thing he did do during the trip was rattle the ice cubes in his glass—constantly. I wondered why, if he disliked the cold so much, he didn't drink his Jack Daniel's neat.

I leaned back as far as I could in the seat and feigned sleep. Gordon's ice cubes bounced. The car purred. I wished Bushy and Pancho were with me, but I had been warned that no animals whatsoever were allowed in the casino—not dogs or cats or canaries or hamsters or turtles or fish . . . not even, I imagine, a pet bumblebee.

The driver spoke only once the entire trip. He asked if we wished to stop at one of the many roadside fast-food restaurants on the Parkway, to use what he assured us were their spanking clean rest rooms. I wondered why a vehicle that offered German *Vogue* and Dom Pérignon hadn't managed to provide its own john.

Luckily, neither Gordon nor I was *in extremis*. And so the long, long limo kept moving over the frozen ground.

About an hour outside of Atlantic City I

did make a concerted effort to make contact with my leading man.

"Have you ever worked with Carlos Weathers?" I asked.

Gordon flung a couple of fresh ice cubes in his glass and poured another drink. "Snot-nosed kid. What does he know?"

I didn't think it was fair to hold Weathers' youth against him. "I hear he's done some very good things in Chicago," I said pleasantly.

Gordon finished his drink and set the empty glass down heavily, as if he were through drinking for the rest of his life. Then he turned and pinned me to the seat with his eyes.

"How long are you in the business?" he asked me. It was an innocuous enough question, but it sounded almost obscene on his lips.

"Nowhere near as long as you," I said.

"Yeah, well . . . you ought to learn how to drink, Cinderella. Before it's all over you'll be doing a lot worse crap than this. I know, see."

I do see, I thought. Gordon Seaver was reminding me that I was not in his league. Just shut up and drink, honey, he was saying. Don't try to match stories with a pro like Gordon Seaver, who's been everywhere and seen everything and could blow his nose on the pathetic salary we'll be getting for this job—

seven days' work at a few hundred dollars over scale. Although perhaps these days Mr. Seaver might be using handkerchiefs like the rest of us. He had to have come down a little in the world, otherwise, what was he doing here with me?

So I didn't speak again on the trip. Neither did Gordon and neither did the driver.

Just after six in the evening the vehicle pulled up in front of the baroque Monte Carlo Casino, at the extreme north end of the Atlantic City boardwalk. It was cold and dark. A fierce wind was coming off the ocean. I could smell the salt water, but I couldn't see anything.

A man came running toward our vehicle, introduced himself as the marketing manager who had arranged the entire thing, Art Agee, and whisked Gordon and me into the hotel.

"Your rooms will be ready in a few minutes. You'll be in our best accommodations, the Winner's Circle, usually reserved for high rollers. Only we don't have very many of those right now. You're on the top floor." He was a confident, very nattily dressed young man. But I really wasn't listening. I was dazzled by the . . . swank . . . of the Monte Carlo. Swank. Like something out of a 1930s film— where was Claudette Colbert in her clingy gold frock by Adrian? Beneath our feet was a long and winding red and gold carpet. Skyward was row upon row upon row of outsized chandeliers, all the same faux crystal, all dripping kitsch. The hotel lobby was circular, with the hotel ringing the outside of the central circle with an atrium. In the center were the gaming pits . . . sunken a bit. From any part of the lobby one could just step down into the casino proper. And from any floor of the inside atrium, where the rooms were, one could gaze down on the gamblers.

Art Agee led us on a whirlwind tour of the casino floor. Through the slot machines and computerized poker setups with their hordes of women—women of all ages, single and in groups, all engulfed in clouds of cigarette smoke and high-pitched chatter—pulling maniacally at the levers, as if in a trance. And into the more "refined" areas, where the blackjack players sat in a sea of plush green velvet, intent on the cards that seemed to be flying from the dealers' fingers. And on to the roulette wheel. And on past the baccarat table. Mr. Agee walked us through the administrative offices behind the cashiers' cage and introduced us briefly to a man called Tobin Haggar, who turned out to be the owner of the casino. Haggar greeted us on the run, so to speak. He was hurrying off to somewhere, and his feet never stopped moving. Still, he managed to come up with a sop to what he must have assumed were our giant show biz egos. "You're grrr-eat," he said warmly. "Really, both of you. Just great. I love your work. Really." And with that he was gone.

"Let's see the theater," Gordon Seaver then said testily.

The marketing manager looked wounded. "You know, Mr. Seaver, we have a brand-new state of the art theater. By any criteria, particularly acoustics, it is superior to anything on or off Broadway."

Gordon arched his eyebrows and all but snorted.

"But," Agee added, "I thought you knew the performances wouldn't be in the main theater."

"Where then?" Gordon asked.

"Follow me. I'll show you."

We trailed behind him as he walked along the lobby. He stopped when he reached what looked like a large bulge in the wall. It turned out to be one of those open bar areas. And in the center was the abbreviated bar itself, its low-lying shelves filled with bottles.

Behind this was a tiny bandstand on which a Latin combo was tuning up.

Gordon was incredulous. "*This* is it? This is where you expect me to perform?"

Us, I thought. Where they expect *us* to perform, Mister Broadway. But I refrained from speaking. I felt a little light-headed. I guess I was tired. I guess I was hungry. Those were the reasons, I'm sure, I was so tempted to laugh. In fact, I turned away from the two of them briefly so that Gordon Seaver would not see me struggling with my mouth.

"On that *fecockteh* bandstand is where I'm appearing!?"

"Well, yes," Art Agee said, genuinely surprised at Gordon's anger. "The bar area seats about a hundred and fifty people . . . well, a hundred or so . . . when filled up . . . on a good night."

Seaver gave me a fleeting glance of utter disgust. Now, he was seeking solidarity with me. Still I said nothing. Our stage wasn't what I had expected either, but I had performed under a lot less commodious circumstances.

"Shall we see if your rooms are ready now?" Agee asked.

We trooped over to the elevator bank. And the moment we stepped into one, Gordon began to mutter: "I hate these things. I hate elevators. And why the hell do they have to make them out of glass? They think that's classy or something? What if you don't *want* to see yourself rising a hundred stories off the ground, huh?"

"There's nothing at all to worry about, Mr. Seaver," Art Agee assured him. "These are state of the art. And they're constantly being maintained."

I wished Art Agee would stop using those words: state of the art.

Gordon Seaver lashed out: "Maintenance won't help if there's a fire. In the fire in Mexico a few years ago, people got roasted to death in the hotel elevators." It was obvious that my leading man had a great fear of flames. In fact, if I had to guess, I'd say Gordon Seaver was a mass of phobias and unreasoning hatreds.

"Yes," Agee countered without skipping a beat, "but their stairwells were locked. Of course we've never had a fire here at the Monte Carlo. But just in case—use the stairs. The doors open easily on each floor, in and out, and they are guaranteed fireproof."

That crisis settled, Art Agee led us to our respective suites.

He had not lied about the accommodations. I'd never stayed in posher quarters. If there was a bed size beyond king, mine was it. All covered in damask and satin. The bathroom was opulent beyond belief—my own whirlpool and fine English soaps and mysterious scented unguents and enormous fluffy bathsheets and robes and theatrical makeup mirrors and boar's hairbrushes and herbal teabags; there were even cable TV and speakers from the stereo system in the main room. I took a look out of my bedroom window. The ocean was there, I could hear and feel it, but it was too dark to see anything but shadows. I noted also the widow's walk on the beachfront window, although it was a fake one with no bottom on which to walk.

At last, Art Agee left me. I undressed quickly and lay down on the bed, then got up to open the window, since they were overdoing the heat a bit. No sooner had I closed my eyes than the phone rang.

It was Gordon Seaver. Did I want to have dinner with him? I did *not*. I'd pegged Gordon for one of those men who feel as if a limb is missing if they don't have a female on their arm at dinner. I thought, with newfound empathy, of the red-haired actress who'd been, I believe, the second Mrs. Gordon Seaver, who now ran a well thought of, if stodgy little restaurant on the Upper East Side of Manhattan, and who drank a bit, I'd heard.

The phone rang again. This time Art Agee was inviting me to supper. Again I declined, showing minimal manners. I really was tired. The truth was, it was too early to sleep. I ordered a ham sandwich from room service, changed into my night things, and picked up the hotel newsletter from the bedstand. I read all about a certain lady from Virginia who had just won a million dollars playing the slot machines.

At nine-thirty I called my niece, Alison.

The cats were fine, she said. Then I phoned Tony Basillio. He wasn't in.

By ten o'clock I was flicking off the lights, and in a matter of minutes was fast asleep.

Four hours later I sat up abruptly, my body bathed in a cold sweat. I swung my legs over the side of the bed, in panic. Where was I? What was happening to me?

Then I realized it had just been a bad dream. I knew where I was.

An evil man had been chasing my two cats, Bushy and Pancho, in a rose-colored tunnel. And they were crying out for my help . . . terrible, pathetic mews.

I gathered my wits. First I had to have a glass of water. And then I had to adjust the thermostat in the room. It was broiling! I might even have mistakenly turned the heat up instead of lowering it earlier.

I got out of bed and walked a little raggedly toward the bathroom.

I heard something!

I stopped walking and held my breath.

There it was again! I *heard* something. I heard a cat mewing!

What was happening? Was I going crazy? The dream was over, wasn't it? I rushed to look under the bed. No. In the closet. No. In the bathroom. No.

Meanwhile the mewing was becoming louder and more pathetic and desperate.

Then I realized it was coming from outside the window I had opened earlier. But how could that be? We were sixteen stories up.

I approached the window slowly. I could see nothing outside. But the sound was definitely coming from out there. Then I quickened my pace and pushed the window open all the way.

A cat jumped into my room. A beautiful, trim, perfectly formed little short hair with fur like spun white gold.

She looked at me and then at her new surroundings. Then matter-of-factly walked to the bed, hopped up, and stretched her little frame out on top of my sheets. The tip of her tail was black and there was a sweet cap of black on her head, between her delicate little ears.

"Who are you?" I asked. "Jean Harlow?"

She paid no attention to me. I went and stuck my head out the window. Where had the cat come from? How was it possible? Was she a stray from the beach who lived under the boardwalk? But how could she climb sixteen floors?

Then I saw the drainpipe that came from the roof and bypassed by a few inches all the fake widow's walks.

I realized there were two possibilities: The cat had either come from the roof and climbed down one story, or had come from the room beneath me and climbed up.

I turned and stared at Harlow. "Well, which is it, girlie? Where'd you come from?"

She yawned expansively and flicked her tail. A very cool feline indeed.

This cat couldn't possibly be a stray. She was much too clean and well groomed. She had to have come from the room beneath. But no pets were allowed in the hotel, Art Agee had told me. He'd been adamant about it, in fact. I thought for a moment. There was no choice. I had to go and find out.

I threw on a bathrobe, told Harlow to stay put, and took the elevator down to the room directly beneath mine. I was so confused and excited that I didn't even realize the inappropriateness of knocking on someone's hotel door at two in the morning.

I needn't have worried, though. The woman who answered did not seem the least bit put out by the intrusion. She was obviously wide awake and altogether friendly.

"What can I do for you?" she asked perkily.

The door had opened immediately after I'd knocked. Standing there in a pair of very expensive silk pajamas I knew the hotel had not provided was a shortish woman in her forties. Around her neck was a woolen muffler and on her feet were big puffy ski boots.

I didn't understand.

I didn't understand the queer way she was dressed. And I didn't understand why the front of her pajamas was stained with blood. Quite a lot of it.

I stepped back instinctively.

"Please. Come in," she said, and moved aside to let me enter.

I wasn't about to do that. But I did look in past her.

On the floor of the room, about ten feet from the door, was another woman. She was naked and there was a lot more blood on her slashed body. It seemed a very safe bet she was dead.

Chapter 2

Casinos clean up messes very fast. And very thoroughly. Even a mess like murder.

Three hours after I saw that poor dead woman on the floor I was back in my suite, resting on an easy chair, my little friend Harlow in my lap.

It was all pretty straightforward:

The laughing woman who had opened the door for me was Carmella Koteit. The dead woman had been a long-time friend of hers—Adele Houghton. They were part of a quartet of friends who met each year to maintain the friendship they'd begun in college more than twenty years ago, at the State University of New York at Stony Brook.

The third friend was Joan Secunda, who was a diet empress, so to speak—the power behind a phenomenally successful chain of diet and fitness clinics.

Bliss Revere completed the quartet. The graceful wife of a wealthy New England businessman, she had turned her considerable intelligence and energy toward projects such as music in the schools and feeding the homeless.

This was the first time any of the women had visited Atlantic City.

As for the crime itself, well, it seemed to have been solved, wrapped up with remarkable dispatch. Carmella Koteit had been arrested for the crime. Although no murder weapon was found, the blood on Carmella's pajamas was determined to be the murdered woman's blood.

Oddly enough, it was the other two friends—Bliss and Joan—who provided the police with the closest thing to a motive Carmella could possibly have had for the killing: an ancient grudge Carmella bore Adele.

It seems Carmella's daughter, many years back, had traveled to the Yucatan on a vacation because Adele had recommended the area. There, the young woman had been killed in a car accident. In her grief over her daughter's death, Carmella had once told Adele and the others she could never forgive Adele. Whether due to the loss of her daughter or some other causes, Carmella had slid deeper and deeper into emotional trouble as the years went on. She had been diagnosed a manic-depressive and had been under a psychiatrist's care for years. The night of the murder, she had obviously slipped into a manic state, which is why she had grinned all during my encounter with her. In fact, when she confessed to the murder, she also quite happily confessed to six other unnamed crimes.

So that was it . . . all wrapped up in three hours. All the blood scrubbed away. All the pillows nice and fluffy again. The onlookers sent away, the cops back to their precinct in Atlantic City, perpetrator in tow. The early-morning gamblers stepping off the buses, in pursuit of their dreams. Business as usual.

And I was sitting with an adorable little cat.

"Did you know her, Harlow?" I asked. "Were you in Adele Houghton's room? Was she your friend, Harlow?"

The lovely little cat burrowed deeper into my lap.

"Was it the blood that frightened you? Was that why you climbed out the window?"

Harlow was saying nothing.

I felt oddly light-headed seated there at five in the morning. As if absolutely nothing had happened. As if it were perfectly natural to have walked into a murder at two in the morning in an Atlantic City casino.

"Should we wait for the sun to come up?" I asked the cat, who fit so comfortably on my lap that I felt I had known her for years.

I played with Harlow's downy ears. What would my cats make of her? Bushy would fall in love. Pancho would have a nervous breakdown.

As my friend Basillio likes to say: "When Alice Nestleton is around one is treated either to a performance or a murder." Too bad Tony wasn't here with me; he would have been treated to both.

I must have fallen fast asleep in that opulent easy chair, because the next thing I remembered was that someone was knocking on my door at seven-thirty in the morning.

I woke with a start and headed for the door.

Then I stopped suddenly.

Where was Harlow?

I had to hide her. She was illegal.

Harlow had, during my long nap, decided to move to the bed. I scooped her up and unceremoniously dumped her into one of the huge closets.

"It will only be for a minute," I assured her.

Then I answered the door.

Art Agee pushed a huge silver room service cart into the room.

"After that terrible experience you had last night, I thought you might need some breakfast," he said, removing the serving cloth.

I also might need some sleep, I thought suddenly.

He had brought fresh juice, muffins, coffee, jams.

"What would you like?" he asked, flipping a napkin over his arm like a waiter.

"Just coffee, please."

He handed me a cup. I put some sugar cubes in. Art Agee looked as if he had just come from his tailor. He was wearing a beautiful gray tweed suit with a deep rich blue shirt and a black tie. My my, this young man was quite a dresser, any time of the day. He had a gorgeous head of carefully combed brown hair, parted on the left. He was lithe but broad shouldered, with a slight hunch. All the features of his face were small—small eyes, small nose, small mouth, small ears, but he was not a small man.

"The muffins are fresh baked."

"No thank you."

I sat back down on the chair and sipped the delicious coffee, listening fearfully for any sounds that would betray Harlow's existence. No, she was blessedly quiet.

I thanked Art Agee again for the breakfast, and waited for him to leave.

He didn't. He began to pace, looking more and more distraught.

Finally he asked me: "Are you *the* Alice Nestleton?"

I laughed out loud. "Well, I surely am *an* Alice Nestleton. There may be others."

"I mean the actress who takes an interest in crime."

I sat up straight. "If you knew that, why did you bring me the coffee and not someone else?"

"You found the body."

"Yes, but if you suspected I was *the* Alice Nestleton, you knew I had seen bloody corpses before. You knew I wouldn't be disabled by what happened . . . you knew I would be able to get my own breakfast."

He didn't reply. He crushed his hands into his jacket pockets.

"What do you want, Mr. Agee?"

"Art. Call me Art."

"Okay. Art it is."

"Carmella Koteit didn't kill her friend. And I want you to find out who did."

"How do you know that?"

"Because I was in Carmella's room last night. And the night before."

I was silent.

He went on: "I left about one in the morning."

"Then that proves nothing."

"But I know she didn't do it."

"How do you know?"

He blurted out: "Because she's a beautiful and kind woman. She's incapable of picking up a knife and murdering anyone with it. Or any other kind of weapon. It's absurd."

"How long have you known her, Art?"

"Two days."

"Hardly a lifetime."

"I know she has some kind of mental disorder. But believe me, she's no killer."

"How did it start?"

"You mean—her and me? Well, I met her in the casino bar. You know, it was one of those things. We ended up in bed. But it was more than sex. We *like* each other. You know—two kindred spirits and all that."

"She's quite a bit older than you, Art."

"Not that much."

He poured more coffee into my cup. His hand was shaking just a bit.

"You have to help—I mean, you have to find out who really killed that woman," he said urgently.

"I'm here to act in love scenes . . . not investigate a murder. Besides, your friend Carmella confessed to the crime."

"She confessed to all kinds of things. She wasn't in her right mind," he said bitterly. Then he started to pace, angrily running his hands through his hair.

"The police even think they know the motive for the murder, Art. She holds the dead woman responsible for her child's death—at least she did at one time. Everyone thought she'd forgiven Adele, but maybe she never has. It's not a run-of-the-mill kind of motive,

27

but a motive nonetheless. Even the murdered woman's friends say so."

Art stopped suddenly and spoke in an impassioned whisper. "I can't have the case go to trial."

"It won't. She confessed to the murder."

"So what? You know that confession won't hold up. Her lawyer will have her retract it. What do they call her? A manic-depressive? They'll plead temporary insanity and fight it. There will be a jury trial. Without the confession there has to be. No weapon was found."

"So?"

"Don't you understand? I'm . . . married."

"Oh."

"Yes. 'Oh.' I have a wife I love. I have two small children I love. I'm sorry about what happened. But I can't let my wife find out. We've had our share of troubles the last couple of years, and she's threatened . . . She'll leave me, I'm telling you. She'll take the children and go if the case comes to trial."

The cat was out of the bag, as they say.

"So what you said at first was a lie. You don't really care about Carmella. It's you you're worried about."

"She didn't murder that woman, Miss Nestleton."

I smiled at him, half in sympathy, half in mistrust.

A very bizarre and very devious trade-off was beginning to form in my head.

"What if I did investigate for you? What will you do for me?"

"I don't have any money."

"I don't want money."

"What, then?"

"I want to be able to keep my cat with me."

"But you can't. No animals are allowed in the rooms."

"That's my price."

"You mean you want to bring your cat here from New York?"

"I don't have to. She's already here."

I walked over to the closet and opened the door. Harlow sauntered out in all her splendor.

Art Agee stared at her as if she were an extraterrestrial. He just didn't know what to say.

"Do we have a deal?" I pressed.

"Yes. Yes." He reached into his jacket and pulled out some keys. He gave them to me. "These are pass keys to the rooms of all four women. Don't use them unless you have to. And if you need help, contact Charlie Lott and tell him you're a friend of mine."

"Who's Charlie Lott?"

"Head of casino security. He comes back from vacation today."

He wheeled the cart out, murmuring as he

exited: "I knew you would help me. I knew you would help me."

After the door closed I rescued Harlow: "Well, I got you a green card," I said.

Then I remembered that Harlow couldn't eat her green card. I ran out into the hall and called Art Agee back.

"I also need some cat food and litter," I whispered.

"It'll be in your room in an hour," he promised. "Remember to keep the DON'T DISTURB sign on the door so the chambermaids won't come in."

I closed the door behind me. I saw that Harlow was so relieved at getting her papers that she had decided to continue her sleep on the bed. It was obvious she wasn't an early riser.

Chapter 3

At two in the afternoon I meandered down to the main floor of the casino. I was wearing a black sweater, jeans, and a long lemon-colored duster.

The moment I stepped out of the elevator I was accosted by a short, powerfully built man, totally bald, with an American flag pin on his lapel.

"Are you Alice Nestleton?" he demanded. And it was an aggressive demand. Involuntarily I shrank back against the wall next to the elevator door.

"I'm Charlie Lott," he announced.

I stared at him. Had Art Agee contacted him and told him to speak to me? I didn't think Art had had sufficient time. Not yet.

"Head of Security," Lott continued.

I nodded that I was aware of who he was.

He glared at me for a long time, but then he suddenly turned sheepish, at last asking meekly: "Can I have your autograph?"

I was flabbergasted.

He pushed a pad and pencil in front of me. "It's for my niece. I collect the autograph of every star who comes to this casino to perform."

Me, a star? It was too much to resist. I grabbed the pencil and signed my name with a flourish. He started to blather about other autographs he had obtained but I saw Gordon Seaver standing by one of the check-in counters waving frantically to me. I excused myself from my admirer and walked over.

Next to Seaver was a man I didn't know. Gordon greeted me and grabbed my arm, propelling me toward the stranger as if I were little Alice being urged to kiss rich Aunt Ethel. "Carlos Weathers, meet Alice Nestleton," he said.

The young director smiled and offered his hand. I shook it.

"When did you get in?" I asked.

He didn't answer, shrugging it off as if it were the kind of question he couldn't be concerned with. I felt a sense of dread. I felt that this young man was going to be trouble—big trouble. He looked like a character out of some corn pone drama: plaid jacket, an ugly tie on a white shirt, and the stupidest high crew cut I have ever seen in my life. It is one of the iron laws of New York theater life that if you have a brilliant director who dresses totally unlike the cliché of a brilliant director—you are in big trouble. Big trouble.

"We should get moving," Carlos Weathers said in a low, urgent voice. I couldn't tell by his speech pattern where he was from. But it sounded a bit foreign, a bit clipped. "We'll meet at nine tonight. A long session. We'll meet in the theater. Management tells me we rehearse there."

Gordon Seaver laughed. "What a joint! We rehearse in the theater and perform in the bar."

"The bar is fine," Carlos Weathers retorted angrily. "I hate enclosed spaces. The bar is open. Open space. Theater is about openness. About freedom."

Gordon Seaver rolled his eyes. Carlos Weathers strode off. Gordon began to talk about the events of the past night and the murder and the hubbub. I made as if I were listening, but I was really listening to the incredible hum of the casino. It seemed like a living presence . . . a low throbbing sound that washed over everything, consisting of people's laughter and croupiers' voices and the shuffle of cards and the clanging of the slot machines and the clanking of glasses as the hostesses in their very scant costumes distributed free drinks to the players.

And the people . . . their faces . . . their forms . . . their outfits fascinated me. Nothing was as I had expected it to be. They had absolutely no style in common. There was no one type of person. It was a real stew of humanity.

Then I saw two women pass close by us and walk out of the casino and onto the frigid boardwalk. One was bundled in a winter white cashmere coat and thigh-high designer boots. The other woman, in her weathered L.L. Bean thermal jacket, had more of the country Superwoman air about her: a woman who could plow a field, shoe a horse, bake bread, raise triplets, run for Congress, all before noon. Both ladies wore impenetrable dark glasses, and they were holding on to each other tightly, as if for dear life.

It was only after they'd gone that I realized the two were Joan Secunda and Bliss Revere—the murdered woman's friends. And the murderer's.

Meanwhile, Gordon had gone silent. He was being stared at by some unfortunately dressed women who had recognized him as a once great Broadway song-and-dance man. They smiled fawningly at him. He smiled back—grimaced really—in that manner unique to a certain kind of celebrity, the kind who obviously both despises and thrives on such attention. And then he headed toward the bar. I walked outside.

The air was bracing cold. The wind was

fierce. I was immediately chilled to the bone. Bliss and Joan were huddled together on one of the benches, two sad, unmoving statues staring out at the deserted beach.

I sat down boldly beside them. Each nodded to me. I said: "I don't know how you stand it out here! It's freezing."

"Anything is better than that horrible place," said Joan.

"Nobody seems to have understood that Adele was murdered last night. Murdered! The people just keep on gambling, feeding those goddamn slot machines and walking around with their greed hanging out obscenely, like nothing had happened," Bliss complained bitterly. "It's disgusting."

"I knew we shouldn't have come here for our get-together. The minute I heard about the idea I knew. This wasn't our kind of place," Joan said. "I mean, just look at this place! It just wasn't us."

"Whose idea was it to come here?" I asked.

"Adele's," said Bliss, taking her friend's hand and beginning to shiver. The wind was actually whistling now, the waves banging crazily against the shore.

"I don't know why she wanted to come here. *It wasn't us*," Joan repeated and looked to me to see if I understood.

"Well," I replied, "everybody likes to unwind a bit."

"Yes. But this isn't our style at all. Look, I don't go around bragging about what I have, but I run a wildly successful business. Bliss here has a fabulous husband and family. She's a contented housewife."

"Don't make me sound quite so much like a cow, darling," Bliss said, in good humor.

"Of course not, darling. You know what I meant." She squeezed Bliss's hand through her glove and went on: "Adele was a good lawyer. A good one. Committed. Caring. Dedicated. And Carmella . . . poor Carmella . . . reviews restaurants for magazines and newspapers, when she can get work.

"Now, take a group of bright women, as diverse as we are—and not one of us gets her kicks gambling. Do you understand? In school we were all interested in music; that's what brought us together in the first place. We started a music society and invited the first all-women's blues band ever to perform at Stony Brook . . . maybe the first ever to perform anywhere. We don't put stupid coins in stupid machines for amusement. We're interested in real life. We're women who read and travel and have things to say and do in the world. Do you understand?" Joan's voice had become shrill, almost crazed.

"Poor Carmella," said Bliss, picking up on her friend's term. "Maybe it was this awful place that deranged her. Maybe the atmosphere in the casino did something to her. Else, why would she stop taking her lithium? She knew what would happen. She was one of those bi-polars who studied their illness. She knew what kinds of dangers she faced."

"What is a bi-polar?" I asked between chattering teeth.

"It's a manic-depressive with wide mood swings . . . wide and chronic. They have to take lithium to keep them from going through the roof and an antidepressant to keep them from going through the floor."

"Well, let's face it," Joan said. "She never was the same after her daughter died. She could never make it after that."

"Did you know Carmella's daughter?" I asked. "The one who died in the Yucatan?"

"Of course we did. She was a lovely young woman," said Joan.

"And she did what she wanted to do. She went where she wanted to go. It was so bizarre that Carmella blamed Adele," noted Bliss.

"But the thing is," Joan said with a growing hurt and anger, "Carmella seemed to have forgotten all about blaming Adele. We've had five get-togethers since her daughter's death and there has never been any trouble at all. It was over and done with, we thought."

She stopped talking suddenly and looked at

me in a confused way as if trying to understand why she was confiding in this total
stranger.

Bliss muttered: "It was this place that did it
to her. Why would she stop taking her med-
ication? It was this place. All this gambling.
All this craziness. There's just something so
corrupt about it, so sleazy."

I wondered whether the two women knew
that Carmella had been sleeping with Art
Agee.

"Did you all keep in touch regularly during
the year?" I asked.

"No. Well, yes and no. We all have busy
lives. We send cards. Once in a while we call.
But the big thing always was this get-together.
Once a year, usually around this time of year.
We all leave what we're doing and who we're
doing it with . . . and we go off together for a
few days. But it'll never happen again, will
it?" Her voice broke into a sort of wail and
she half cried out: "Will it?"

I looked at the mighty Atlantic. It was no
longer green. It seemed, as the afternoon
lengthened, to become a dark metal blue with
glints of purple. And the froth of the waves
seemed gray and dirty.

"Did she have a cat?" I asked.

"Did who have a cat?" asked Joan.

"Adele."

"No."

"Are you sure?"

"Yes. But where do you mean? At her apartment? In her room?"

If the answer was no, why was the woman trying to pin me down? I didn't know. "Either place," I replied.

"No cat," said Joan.

"I remember no cat," said Bliss.

"I don't remember her even talking about a cat," added Joan.

I stood up and leaned against the rail. My eyes swept down the boardwalk . . . a row of casinos, each one grander than the last, each freakier in its desperate attempt to distinguish itself from all the rest. All of the casinos had at least one entrance and one exit onto the famous Atlantic City boardwalk. But the boardwalk itself was decrepit and grim. And the tiny abandoned stores between casinos were like a forest of sore thumbs.

"How long will you be staying here now?"

"As soon as the police say we can go, we will go," said Joan.

"But what about Carmella?" Bliss added. There was no answer.

I walked back into the casino, leaving the two friends still clutching each other in their misery.

I walked quickly through the hotel lobby and took the elevator back up to my room to check on Harlow.

She had eaten every morsel of her food and was now perched on the table near the large television set.

I sat down across from the nodding kitty. "You want to hear something strange, Harlow? I don't have any problem accepting the police and almost everyone else's version of the murder. It seems right to me, from beginning to end. The problem is you. You're the mystery. Who are you and where do you come from?"

Chapter 4

It was one minute past nine in the evening and the three of us sat in the theater—a beautifully appointed 465-seat house. The lights were on. The stage was empty. We were alone, seated in the first three seats of the first row.

Carlos Weathers seemed to be lost in thought, his body thrust forward on the seat, his face between his hands. I looked at Gordon Seaver. He shrugged his shoulders. We waited until the brilliant director had gathered his thoughts.

Finally Weathers sat back with a flourish, saying: "Okay. Here is what I want to do." Then he leaped up from the chair, walked toward the stage, turned violently, and squatted down like a football coach speaking to his players.

"I think we should blow them out of the casino," he said conspiratorially. "I think we should provide them with theater they have never experienced before."

I shifted uncomfortably in my seat. I didn't know where this was going, but I knew already I didn't like it. This young man was really going to be trouble. I thought it best to head him off now—at the pass.

"Look, I don't know what you're thinking of," I said, "but please remember that for the most part our audience are middle-class, middle-aged people who just want a little Valentine's Day nostalgia with their roulette and prime ribs. At least that's the way I read it."

I looked to Gordon for support, but he was staring at the ceiling.

"Yes, yes, I understand what you're saying, Alice. I know we're all here for a quick paycheck. But that's when great theater happens. Suddenly. Off the cuff. Under the most lurid circumstances. Get it, Alice?"

I wanted to crawl under the seat. And I really *didn't* like the way he pronounced my name—Al-isss, with a hiss. But I said nothing.

"Here's our project," he announced, and then gave weight to his statement with a long pause, as if cueing us to lean forward in our seats in breathless anticipation. I wanted to shoot the fool right then and there.

"*Sweet Bird of Youth*," he announced triumphantly.

Neither Gordon nor I said a word.

"And the mad scene from *Hamlet*, it goes without saying. Ophelia's mad scene."

Gordon made a sound, a kind of pitiful moan. I'd heard that sound before: Pancho, my hooligan cat. When I put him on my lap and pin him on his back and gather his four legs into a little bundle and sniff his nose.

Carlos Weathers, besotted with his own genius, stood up straight and proud, waiting for our plaudits, I supposed.

"But I thought we were doing love scenes," I said slowly, calmly.

"And aren't we? Weren't you listening, Alisss?"

"A relationship between an aging drunk film star and a young—well, a young stud—is hardly what the management of this casino would consider a Valentine's Day theatrical program for their guests," I said.

"Let me decide what a love story is. Besides, we're here to shake these people up. To give them a slice of theater they will never forget."

"Besides," I kept right on, "Gordon is a fine actor, but he doesn't look like a young Paul Newman, and that's what the role requires."

"Meaningless."

"They'll fire us after the first performance," I warned.

"You New York actresses are all alike," he said dismissively, "so damn unimaginative."

That tore it! I blew up. I told him what he could do with his ridiculous idea. Then I quit! On the spot. And stomped out, heedless of what kind of exit I was making.

Once in the hotel lobby, I started to breathe deeply because I was so furious my whole body was shaking. I began to walk around the long, circular lobby, trying to rein in my fury.

I must have walked around the enormous casino pit about three times before I started to calm down. And then I realized what I had done, how stupid I had been.

Why had I gotten so upset? It would be only five days of nonsense and I needed the money very bad. What had come over me? I had dealt with crazy directors all of my life and I never had blown up at them so quickly, so totally.

I had to get myself together. I stepped down from the lobby into the casino pit and sat at the first seat I saw—in front of a video poker machine. Yes, I had to calm down. I had to think.

"When I get that upset, young lady, I play *two* machines instead of one."

I turned to my right. Next to me was seated a tall, thin, elderly black woman wearing a dark cloche hat and a vintage beaded dress.

She was staring at the machine, but she had obviously spoken to me.

"But I'm not interested in gambling," I said.

"This isn't gambling," she said. "It's winning and losing. That's all. I like winning. I like losing. I lose all the time. It makes me feel good. I take the bus in from Philadelphia every day. It's so calm and nice here. Losing is wonderful. As long as you do it right."

I laughed.

"See there," she said, "you're doing better already." Then she asked, "What do they call you?"

"Alice Nestleton."

"I am Evie Soames and it is a pleasure."

"Same here."

She leaned over and put a half-dollar piece into the machine in front of me.

"Now press that button," she said.

"Which button?"

"The one that says PLAY."

I pushed the button. Five cards came up. Two three's. A king. A seven. A four.

"What do I do now?"

"Press the HOLD button under each of the threes."

I did as she said.

"That means you'll draw three cards."

I waited; nothing happened.

She laughed. "No, you have to press the PLAY button again."

So I did it.

All hell broke loose. Bells rang. Gongs went off. Evie Soames clapped her hands.

"What is going on?" I asked, jumping up from my seat.

"You don't know?"

"No."

"Well, just press that button on the side," she said.

Again, I obeyed her. Coins began cascading out of the machine like a belching volcano.

Then I looked at the video screen. Pictured there were three threes and two jokers.

"Young lady," Evie said delightedly, "you have five of a kind. Five threes. Because those two ugly fellas are jokers and jokers are wild."

When the deluge ended, I counted the loot. Four hundred coins had come tumbling out of that machine.

"I think I need a drink," I said. I looked at Evie Soames. "May I buy you a drink also?"

"Delighted," the old woman said. She then helped me load the coins into a cardboard bucket and then redeem them for paper money.

We walked into one of the many theme cafes that ringed the lobby. This one had a country-western motif. Evie and I ordered barbecued chicken sandwiches and bottles of ale.

"Young lady," said Evie Soames, "if this is really your first time gambling, you should consider a career in the field. Five of a kind is most impressive."

"I have enough trouble being an actress," I replied.

Evie waved my objection away. "You may be," she said, "another Cleopatra."

"Who is Cleopatra?" I asked, assuming that my new friend was not talking about the Egyptian queen.

"A famous gambler in Atlantic City. She goes from casino to casino and always wins. Her specialty is blackjack."

"Why doesn't she play what I played? Too noisy?"

"Well, young woman, a lot of people who play blackjack or shoot craps don't like machine games. There's no human contact."

"That doesn't bother you, does it?"

"Not at all. I love to sit down in front of one of those video poker machines and slip my quarter or half in and let all probability bust loose."

It was such an odd expression that I must have screwed up my face in perplexity.

"You don't know what I mean, do you, young woman?"

"Not really."

"Do you know how many possibilities there are? I mean in the number of hands that can

47

come up on screen. Just a regular video poker machine with no deuces wild or jokers wild."

"A lot, I guess. After all, there are fifty-two cards in a deck."

"The number is 2,598,960."

"That is astonishing. I had no idea it was that many."

Evie Soames's eyes were twinkling. She looked for a moment like a mad scientist. "Now what would happen if I played 2,598,960 straight games? Would I get a chance to see every possible combination?"

"I don't know. I don't think so."

"Of course not. Every hand is a new deal. You can get the same hand on the screen a hundred straight times, in theory. In fact, I once read a book that said if you want to experience every possible hand in a video poker machine, you would have to play a game every ten seconds of every minute of every hour for more than three hundred days straight. And there is still no guarantee."

"That is a lot of video poker," I said.

"One billion three hundred million games to be exact." She giggled like a young girl. "How I do love those wild numbers!"

"Then what's the point of playing video poker at all?" I asked. "It seemed so easy at the time," I added, savoring now the memory of the bells going off and the coins beginning to erupt.

"It *is* easy. That's why so many people play video poker. It gives the player the best shot at winning in the whole casino."

"But what about all those figures you're throwing around?"

"Those are possibilities . . . not odds."

"I'm not sure I follow."

"The odds themselves are good. Less than five to one for a 'jacks or better' pair. Less than fourteen to one for three of a kind. And not only are the odds good but the payoff is good."

"You mean how much you win?" I felt very unsure of what she was saying. This was a whole new world to me.

"Exactly. For two pair you triple your money. And that rises progressively until you get paid eight hundred coins for every one coin you play for the Big One."

"What is the 'Big One'?"

"Ah. The Big One is . . . the Big One," she said cryptically. She sipped her ale and lit up one of those impossibly long and ridiculously thin cigarettes. Then she said: "The Big One is a royal flush. The odds against getting one are forty thousand to one. But it happens. Yes, indeed, it happens."

"Maybe," I suggested, "that famous lady gambler you mentioned—the one who wins all the time—maybe she won the Big One so often she grew tired of the game."

Evie found that very amusing. "It's possible. Anything is possible with that Cleo."

"By the way, why is she called Cleopatra?"

"Because she wears one of those Egyptian-style wigs—long black hair with bangs. Like Miss Taylor wore in the movie. And because her luck comes from stroking a mysterious cat. At least that is what she says."

I laughed out loud. It was good to laugh again. This old woman had totally defused my rage against Carlos Weathers.

"Well," I said, "the comparison is flattering and I certainly have enough cats in my life to keep me busy stroking—but I think I'll retire from gambling. I'll go out a winner."

"What are you doing here if you don't gamble?" Evie asked.

"As I said, I'm an actress. And I was hired to play some love scenes on Valentine's Day."

"How nice!"

"Yes. But when I sat down next to you I had just resigned."

"No wonder you were so upset."

"But thanks to you I think I'll go back and unresign."

"Good. Then I'll be able to see your play."

I left Evie in the restaurant and went out into the lobby to call Gordon Seaver's room. He answered. First off, I apologized to him. Then I told him I'd call Carlos Weathers and tell him I was ready to go back to work. Gordon said I shouldn't worry—Weathers had not taken the resignation seriously anyway. He knew "how actresses were." Gordon was still laughing when he told me "Good night, Princess," using the name of the character from the Tennessee Williams play.

"Good night, Chance," I retorted. He sure as hell was no Paul Newman. But then I was no Geraldine Page.

I went back to join my newfound friend and we devoured our chicken sandwiches and drank the ale to the last drop.

Chapter 5

It was very lucky that I decided to do what Carlos Weathers wanted me to do—to just resign myself to his madness. Because the next morning, at six A.M., at rehearsal, he announced something even more bizarre. Not only were we going to do inappropriate scenes; he had come up with the added conceit that we would treat them as workshop exercises.

"You see, Alice, I am very glad you reconsidered. I am very glad you overcame your anger. We need each other. We are going to show these people what theater is. We are going to take them to the heart of the matter—two actors and a director peeling the onion . . . the onion of love . . . on stage, in front of them."

As I said, he could tell me anything. I had decided on doing the seven days and getting the money. It didn't matter how delusional that fool was.

As for Gordon Seaver, I truly think he found it funny. It confirmed his well-earned cynicism that there were only two kinds of directors—opportunists and madmen. And it appeared that Gordon and I had before us one of the rare examples of both in one living person—Carlos Weathers.

Carlos laid out for Gordon and me just what scenes in *Sweet Bird of Youth* we were going to deal with, how we were going to compensate for lack of props, what he was going to highlight, how we must totally ignore the audience to make it appear like a true workshop production, how we must intersperse the production with authentic questions we have, so that the audience realizes that the dramatic scene itself is a vehicle for the performer's enlightenment. On and on he went. Crazier and crazier. It was all compounded by the fact that Carlos Weathers, once he was working, could not simply talk to you in a straightforward manner. He had to continually crouch or pirouette or wheel. One got exhausted just following the movements.

But finally the meeting was over and I, stupefied, wound my way back down the corridor, to the elevators and up to my room.

"Harlow," I said to the lovely cat on my bed, "you don't know what aggravation is. Yes, I know it must have been tough getting here.

53

But believe me, you have never met anyone like Carlos Weathers. And I truly believe you're too much of a lady to even deal with him."

There was a knock on the door. I shivered, imagining for a moment that it was Carlos Weathers, coming up to lecture me some more on his theories of performance.

But it wasn't Weathers. It was Art Agee.

And the moment I saw his pale face framed in the doorway I felt absolutely terrible, because I hadn't done a damn bit of criminal investigation other than talking to the two friends of the murder victim on the boardwalk. In fact, to be honest, I hadn't been thinking about the dead woman or her arrested friend at all. And that was a shame. That was gross. Maybe the casino cleans out minds as well as pockets.

What if he, Art Agee, decided that I wasn't holding up my half of the bargain and Harlow had to go? I couldn't let her go until we found out where she wanted to go or where she had come from.

Nervously, I ushered him into the room. He must be angry at me, I thought.

He stared at the cat for what seemed the longest time. Then he walked to the window and stared out at the ocean.

"I have something to tell you," he finally declared.

I burst out laughing. He looked at me sternly. I felt ashamed of myself for laughing at him, but the way he had spoken those words and the words themselves for some odd reason reminded me of a Sunday School teacher I had in Minnesota. A very heavyset lady who started out the first class with those exact words: "I have something to tell you."

And tell us she did. "If you want to be heaven bound," she intoned, "you have to turn Satan down. It's as simple as that."

I don't know why he reminded me of that teacher.

"I'm sorry for laughing, Art. I just remembered something."

Art brushed it all aside with a savage chop of his right hand.

"Something very bad happened last night," he said.

"What?"

"Someone broke into their rooms, at about four in the morning."

"Whose rooms?"

Adele's—the dead woman. And Carmella's and the other two friends as well."

"Was anyone hurt?"

"No. Adele is dead, if you remember. Carmella is in custody. And it seems that the two others so hate this place they stayed in a motel and came back at six this morning. That's when they found the mess."

"Do you think it was a hotel employee?" I offered.

"Why would I think that?"

"Well, someone who knew the rooms were empty and was looking for jewelry or cash or other valuables."

"A hotel employee would know that the guests, at least most of them who are well-heeled, put their valuables in safe-deposit-boxes during their stay here. Besides, whoever went in those rooms was looking for something specific. They trashed the rooms. They even broke into a wall. And they didn't touch whatever few valuables there were."

Harlow leaped lightly off the bed and went under it. She didn't like Art Agee's tone of voice, obviously.

"It gets worse," Art said.

"How so?"

"Those two friends of Carmella's and Adele's have accused you of the break-in of their rooms."

"Me?"

"Yes. They said you followed them and asked all kinds of strange questions."

"I did speak to them. As you know, Art, you asked me to conduct a criminal investigation."

"Don't lie to me, Miss Nestleton. Did you do it?"

"Don't be foolish, Art. You yourself gave me the keys. Why would I have to break in?"

"I know, but—"

"No."

"Okay. I believe you. What do we do now?"

"Do you want me to continue the investigation?"

"Yes."

"Do you want me to intensify the investigation? Because to be quite honest, Art, I have been going slowly. The whole thing has seemed to me kind of unreal."

"Damn it. You saw the goddamn slashed body first. How could it be unreal?"

A point well taken. "I asked you a question, Art."

"Yes. Yes. Intensify the investigation. Invigorate the investigation. Illuminate the investigation. Words! By any means necessary, Miss Nestleton!"

He was working himself up into a terrible state. I thought he might lose control completely if I didn't do something, so I held up my hand, signaling that he ought to slow down, and I pressed a glass of cold water into his hands.

"Listen to me, Art. I want you to take me to Adele's safe-deposit box . . . if she had one."

"Are you serious?"

"Quite serious. If you want me to prove that your girlfriend—"

"She's not my girlfriend," he interrupted harshly.

"If you want me to prove that Carmella did not murder her friend . . . then you are going to have to help me get a look in that box. Doesn't it make sense, Art? Particularly after someone broke into her room last night looking for something."

"It wasn't only *her* room they broke into. And besides, no one can get into those safe-deposit boxes."

I smiled and waited.

"I don't even know if Adele had such a box," he protested.

"Why don't you find out, Art, and let me know. I'll be here, taking a nap. The rehearsal was fatiguing."

He hesitated. He started to leave. He stopped. Then he said: "Wait for me here! I'll find out. Give me about a half hour." Then he was gone.

"You can come out now, Harlow," I said. "The bad man is gone."

Harlow crawled out, a bit ruffled and disgusted.

I lay down on the bed. I knew . . . I felt in my bones, as my grandmother used to say . . . that my indifference and my dilettantism was about to come back to haunt me. The theatrical misadventure was bad enough. But now I had the distinct feeling that Atlantic City was about to become downright unhealthy. In fact, compared to what I feared might be coming, Carlos Weathers was starting to look a lot like John Houseman.

Art Agee didn't return in half an hour. He was away more than two hours. But I didn't care, because I had a wonderful nap with a wonderful dream accompanying it. In the dream, Harlow the cat came on stage with me dressed as Joan of Arc. As grand inquisitor, I really got to chew the scenery, and in the end we both received a thunderous ovation.

When the marketing manager finally did enter my room again he had somehow transformed himself into a ridiculous version of a secret agent. I mean, the young man was so tense and sweating and so clandestine that he really frightened me for a while.

"If it upsets you so much, let's forget about it," I said.

"No! No! It's all set. The whole thing is done. But we have to do it fast. And we have to keep out of sight."

Off we went into the hallway, but we didn't take the usual elevator. We walked to the extreme far end of the hall and went down in a much smaller and plainer elevator.

We emerged in some kind of basement with

corridors. Art began to walk very fast. I followed close behind him. We passed what seemed to be the kitchens of the various restaurants in the hotel, and then rooms filled with enormous washing and drying machines. It was very chilly in the corridors, as if we were just under the street.

We reached a dead end . . . a large copper door. Art banged on it heavily. It opened, and an old man in a hotel security uniform led us into a small file room. In the center was a table, a phone, and a chair.

"Wait there," Art ordered. I sat down. "It will arrive in a minute. You have five minutes. I'll be waiting outside." And then he left.

I waited patiently. It was, at least, warm in this small room.

The old man brought in the safe-deposit box and laid it on the table. Then he left.

It looked no different from the safe-deposit boxes you would rent in a bank . . . except it was a bit larger. And it didn't have the simple latch opening; it had a kind of twist mechanism, like the clasp on a change purse.

When I finally did get the knack of the twist and opened the lid, all I could see was one of those old heirloom pins that every grandmother wills her granddaughter—a cameo. But when I reached back in the box I could feel other objects.

I raised the box, inclined it, and shook all the items down the slope.

There was a lovely silver pen and pencil set wrapped in velvet and secured with a string. And there was a sewing kit with a 14-karat thimble.

Finally, I found an elongated Victorian-era ladies gold mesh bag with a delicate chain handle.

I opened the purse and pulled out a crumpled object. It took me a minute to identify it. It was a raven black wig.

There were other, smaller things in the purse. I shook them out. Strange, circular medallions that were also foreign to me at first, until I remembered seeing them on the gaming tables when Art Agee took Gordon Seaver and me on that short tour of the casino. They were gambling chips. Twelve of them.

I stuffed the objects back into the purse and thrust the purse under my sweater.

Then I closed the box and waited.

The old man came in and retrieved the box without a word. Then Art Agee bounced in and led me out of the room and back through the morass of basement corridors.

"Did you find anything?" he asked urgently.

"Not a thing of interest," I lied.

We reached the lobby. "What next?" he asked.

"I'll let you know," I replied. "Just be patient a while longer."

He threw up his hands and then walked away. I waited until he was out of sight and then walked swiftly to the rim of the casino and looked around.

Yes, my friend Evie Soames was in her usual place—at her favorite video poker machine.

I walked into the casino and sat down next to her. She smiled her greeting and tapped the machine in front of me.

"No," I said emphatically, "but I need your help."

"They say good help is hard to find these days," she said. But she smiled.

"Look at this," I said, holding up one of the chips I had found in the safe-deposit box.

She sat back.

"What are these, Evie?"

" 'What are they,' she asks! Are you pulling my very old leg, young lady? Are you really telling me you don't know what that is?"

"I know it's a chip."

"Oh, it's more than a chip. It's a one-hundred-dollar chip from the casino down the road—Castles."

"And what is this?" I asked, shaking the wig out and putting it on my head.

"My, my, my," Evie said, "you look just like Cleopatra."

"That's what I was afraid of," I said.

Was Adele, the murdered woman, really the legendary lady gambler with the Cleopatra wig? Was Harlow the gambler's mysterious cat? If so—the script had to be rewritten.

Chapter 6

It was two o'clock in the afternoon when Evie Soames and I exited the Monte Carlo and strode out resolutely on the frigid boardwalk to the neighboring casino called Castles.

She had agreed to guide me there along with my wig and chips. In fact, she seemed to be anticipating a great adventure.

I also carried with me a picture of Adele and her three friends that had been taken their first night in the hotel. One of the ubiquitous camera girls who constantly prowled about with their Instamatics, charging a mere fifteen dollars a developed shot, had snapped the photo as the women ate dinner that evening. Art Agee had quickly obtained it for me from Charlie Lott, the head of casino security.

If anyone was looking for camera subjects, I'm sure Evie and I made for an interesting snap as we walked on the boardwalk from one casino to the other. A tall, middle-aged blond woman and a taller and thinner old black lady, braving the elements and clutching at each other's coat as if to prevent the other from being blown into the Atlantic. The wind kept blowing Evie's hat askew, but she happily adjusted it, again and again.

As we stepped inside the revolving door of Castles, Evie Soames confided in me: "I used to play here quite a bit, but you know, the bathrooms just weren't as nice as they are over at the Monte Carlo."

Once inside, I was startled to see that except for minor configurations, it was exactly the same as the casino I had just left. Either one had copied the other or both had copied a third casino, or perhaps, more intelligently, there was one master archetype casino.

We stood on the cusp of the casino pit and stared out over the assembled, like travelers from a different land. I heard Evie sigh deeply, as if it were, indeed, a beautiful sight.

"Where would Cleopatra be playing?" I asked.

"Well, you found hundred-dollar chips, so she probably was playing blackjack at the hundred-dollar minimum table. The tables run from a five-dollar minimum to a hundred-dollar minimum. Not too many people play for those high stakes."

"Can you walk me by those tables?"

"Sure," she answered, but a bit wary.

"How do I look?" I asked her.

"Pretty as a picture."

I laughed and quickly wrapped a rubber band around my hair, gathering it into a fluffy tail. Then I slipped Cleopatra's wig on.

"Still pretty as a picture?"

"I hope you know what you are doing, young lady," she said.

Together we sauntered into the casino area.

"There they are," Evie whispered.

There were only three blackjack tables that featured hundred-dollar minimums. They were set off from the others as if to accentuate their eliteness.

Two of the tables had two players each in addition to the dealer. The third table had only one player.

"What are you going to do?"

"Just walk by, Evie, just walk by." And that is what we did, slowly.

"Now what?" Evie asked.

"We walk by thrice," I said dramatically, using that archaic term "thrice" because I thought it would appeal to Evie Soames, who, I believed, was a church lady, when she wasn't gambling, that is.

So we walked back and forth three times, passing slowly and deliberately in front of each of the one-hundred-dollar-minimum tables. The players of course couldn't care who or what walked by. The dealers, who were facing us, each gave us a glance and then proceeded.

"Now what?" Evie asked, after our third run.

"Just keep looking over my shoulder and let me know if any of the dealers do anything strange."

Evie adjusted her spectacles and stared out. "Nope," she said after about ten seconds. "Nothing happening." She kept looking. "Nope . . . nope . . . Wait!"

"Just tell me what's happening, Evie."

"One of the dealers is signaling the pit boss. Yes. He's getting relieved. He's standing up. He's leaving."

"Which one?"

"The young man. The one with the long hair."

"Where is he going?"

"I'm watching. . . . He's walking out of the pit. . . . Now he's lighting a cigarette. . . . Ah, he's going into the coffee shop."

"Let's go, Evie," I whispered urgently.

The young man was seated disconsolately at a small table, puffing furiously and staring down at an untouched cup of coffee.

We approached. In a single motion I removed the wig and plopped it onto the table next to his cup. He recoiled.

Then he glared at me. "Who are you? What do you want?"

"May we sit?" I asked.

He didn't answer.

Not bothering to ask permission again, Evie and I joined him in the booth.

"You knew her, didn't you?" I asked.

"What are you trying to prove with this nonsense?" he whispered angrily, pushing the wig back at me.

I calmly introduced Evie and myself to the young man. He was very thin, his face sharp angled and haunted, disconcertingly hand-some.

He mumbled his name: "Lyle Sweetnum."

And then he was silent. For the longest time the three of us stared down at the un-touched coffee. If he was so upset, he could have left, but he didn't. He could have called for help from Security. He could have done a hundred things, but all he did was sit there.

Then I slid out the photograph and pushed it across the table toward him. "That is she, isn't it? Cleopatra. Without the wig." With his spoon I tapped on Adele's face.

He stared at the photo. Then he nodded. "I heard she was murdered," he said sadly.

I felt a sharp kick under the table. Evie was signaling me.

Yes, I told her with my eyes. Yes, I know: any reports of a murder in the Monte Carlo would say that a guest named Adele

Houghton was dead, not Cleopatra the gambler.

Sweetnum seemed to be struggling to breathe. "She was a wonderful woman. She helped me out with money. Everybody thinks we dealers make a fortune. We make peanuts. We are dependent on tips. She knew that. She helped me out." He started playing with the cup. "I hear they got the killer. I hope they boil her in oil."

"Tell me what you know about her," I pressed.

"What is there to know? She was a wonderful woman who lived in Atlantic City. She gambled a lot. She always won. She was generous."

"No. She didn't live in Atlantic City. She lived in Manhattan. She was a labor lawyer by profession."

"Don't tell me what I know. She lived in Atlantic City."

"Do you have proof of that?"

"She told me. She told me she lived a few blocks from this casino."

He picked up the wig and played with it.

Then his voice dropped and he spoke in a torrent of words . . . impassioned: "I told her to shut up about that cat of hers. I told her to keep quiet. I told her if she kept talking like that someone would kill her for the cat."

"What was she saying?"

69

"That her cat made her a winner. That her cat was a magic charm. That she never lost because she stroked her wonderful cat."

"But who would believe such nonsense?"

"I did."

"Oh, come now, Mr. Sweetnum. You're a dealer. A professional. I'd have thought you knew better. That gambling is about mathematical odds, luck . . . whatever. But not about stroking a cat."

"I never believed it until I met her. Now I truly do believe it. I truly do."

His affirmation of the occult brought back a memory to me; of Adele's two friends—Joan, the entrepreneur, and Bliss, the overeducated housewife—huddled together on the boardwalk like witches in Ray•Bans, like two spooky mob widows.

They had seemed to me at the time two rational, middle-aged, middle-class women who were in a state of grief.

But perhaps they knew of Adele's double life. Perhaps they knew of hundred-dollar chips. Perhaps they knew everything, things I hadn't even glimpsed, and, despite their backgrounds and their level of education, decided to make a wager on murder. Kill the friend. Grab the cat. Let Carmella take the fall. Were they that stupid? Is it possible for educated women to be that stupid? And then to have the cat escape! And run into the protective arms of Aunt Alice.

Lyle Sweetnum stood up abruptly. "I have to get back to the tables. I don't know who you people are and I don't care. But I want you to know that the lady who wore that wig was something special." And then he was gone.

When he had left I asked Evie Soames, "Can you show me where to cash in the twelve chips?"

"Yes."

"Good. Because after you show me that, I'm going to show *you* something."

"What's that?" Evie asked.

"Her cat."

"You don't mean Cleopatra's cat?"

"Yes."

"You mean, you *have* her?"

"That's right. She's waiting for us right now. And if I'm any judge, she's going to find you as much of a blessing as I do."

Chapter 7

It is very hard to describe the scene—it was filled with absurdities and over it all hovered what can only be called an unreal presence.

But let me set the scene.

My casino room. Harlow was on the bed.

One side, me. The other side, Evie Soames. Both seated on the edge of the bed, bookends for Harlow.

Further back on the bed, near the pillows, were twelve hundred-dollar bills folded and held together with a clip. It was the money from the redeemed chips.

"So that's the cat," Evie said in wonderment. She had said the same thing maybe twenty times since she came into the room and saw Harlow.

"Yes. That is the cat," I replied, as I had replied to her twenty previous comments. "The face that launched a thousand chips."

"She is beautiful," Evie said.

"Yes. One of the most beautiful cats I have ever seen," I affirmed.

"What kind is she?"

"I haven't the slightest idea. Mostly short hair, I think, and a bit of Persian, and just the slightest trace of Siamese about the eyes and ears."

"She does look like Miss Jean Harlow," Evie confirmed.

"Yes. I think it is a good name."

We were, of course, just dancing around the edges. We were just crawling up to the real matter at hand because we were both frightened.

Finally I could bear it no longer. "Tell me the truth, Evie. Do you believe it?"

"Let me put it this way: I *think* I do."

"Evie, you're one of the most sensible people I've ever known. Yet you're telling me you believe that a woman can consistently beat the most skilled professional gamblers in the world just by stroking a cat for luck?"

"Yes, I think I believe that," she said, and then she bent forward and very gently reached out and touched one of Harlow's paws.

"Well, I don't know what to believe. It sounds ridiculous. It sounds like one of those phenomena that you simply can't prove or disprove. It's all smoke."

I leaned over and scratched Harlow's flank.

She purred. "Isn't that right, Sugarpuss?" Her magnificent tail waved.

I stared suddenly at Evie. She was smiling. I didn't appreciate the smile. It was as if she was making fun of me; as if she didn't believe what I was saying.

"There is a way," she said.

"A way to what?"

"To see if it is smoke or not."

"How?"

She got up from the bed and walked to her purse, which was on the dresser. She removed a pack of playing cards and brought them back to the bed. She held them up to me.

"I don't understand," I said.

"First I'll teach you blackjack," said Evie. "Then you'll stroke this cat. Then you'll go down to the casino."

It was breathlessly elegant. I stared at Harlow. I looked at the deck of cards. I squirmed. I fidgeted. I walked about. I felt stupid but also oddly scientific, as if I were evaluating an empirical protocol.

Evie opened the deck and began the Evie Soames short course in the art and science of blackjack playing.

She quickly showed me the point of the game—the points of the cards in your hand have to have a total that is closer to the number 21 than the cards in the hand of the dealer. She showed me how to "hit"—that is, tap the table to indicate the desire for another card. And how to "stand"—silently gesturing with the hand that no more cards are wanted.

She outlined the basic casino rules—the dealer must "hit" if his own hand contains 16 or under, and stand if his hand totals 17 or more.

She demonstrated to me how to split cards and double down.

We played a few practice hands with her acting as dealer. Then she said: "You're ready."

"Is that all I have to know?"

"Look, Alice, hundreds of books have been written about blackjack. There are all kinds of theories and ways to play the game—counting strategies, betting strategies, anything to tip the odds away from the house. But you don't need any of that."

"Why not? I'm going to play for money."

"Because you have Harlow," she said.

"I don't feel confident."

"There's nothing to be frightened of. It's a very cut-and-dried game."

"But can't you give me some kind of system?"

"You mean like the real gamblers use?"

"Yes. So I don't get confused. If I get confused, it won't be a test of anything except my own foolishness."

"Well," Evie said, "the only system that really works is the counting system. And if they find out you're a 'counter'—the casino won't take kindly to it."

"The casino's affection doesn't really interest me," I said a bit testily.

"If you want to try to use the counting system, I'll show it to you."

"First tell me what it is."

"The theory behind it is very simple." She paused, smiling, as if she were contemplating a recipe for a beautiful dish. "Every time you sit down at the blackjack table, the house, the dealer, has an advantage, because if you have a seventeen-point hand and the dealer has a seventeen-point hand, the dealer wins. The dealer always wins a tie. But, the player in blackjack has something on his side that no other casino player has."

"What?"

"Well, every time you flip a pair of dice you have the exact same odds of rolling a seven—namely, five to one. And every time you put a coin into a video poker machine you have the exact same odds of being dealt a flush."

"Why doesn't that apply to blackjack? It's just a card game. There are fifty-two cards in the deck."

"First of all, because they play with several

decks. But most important, because the odds change as the deck is diminished. The odds change after each hand is played, as the deck becomes smaller."

"That makes sense."

"So all you have to do is remember the cards that have already been played."

"Why?"

"Ah! Because if the cards in the deck that haven't been played contain an abundance of high-point cards—tens, pictures, or aces—you have a better chance to win. And if the remaining cards have an abundance of low-point cards, the dealer has a better chance to win."

"This is getting very complicated, Evie."

"You asked for it, honey."

"Can't you just tell me the way to do it? I'll take your word that it works."

"Oh, it does work, most of the time. As you're playing and counting, and you see that a lot of small cards have already been played and you know that there are a lot of big cards left in the deck—you increase your bets."

"Can I jot them down on a pad?"

She burst out laughing. "No! You have to keep it in your head. During every hand you watch the cards carefully. When a card comes up that is less than ten, you remember '*plus one.*' Any card ten points or more—remember '*minus one.*' At the end of the round, you total. If the total yields a *plus*, that means a lot of small cards have left the deck and a lot of those good fat ones are remaining. So . . . poof! . . . you bet big!"

All those pluses and minuses were making my head spin. "Where did you learn all this, Evie?"

"Here and there, honey. Here and there."

"It sounds crazy."

"The cards don't lie, young woman."

It was just too much for me. As of late I had trouble remembering even my room number. "I just don't think I can handle it, Evie," I confessed.

She sighed a little.

And we both looked over at Harlow.

So, the time had come to do the voodoo, mojo, kabbalistic ritual.

"You think I should say any words?" I asked Evie.

"You mean like prayers?"

"Yes."

"Well, I don't see how the Twenty-Third Psalm can hurt you."

That was too much. I couldn't do that. I picked Harlow up and hugged her.

Then, holding her with my right hand, I began to stroke her with my left hand. Once. Twice. Three times. Up to eleven times. Why eleven? I don't know. But it was eleven. Then

I dropped her back down onto the bed. She seemed quite happy at the stroking.

"Do you feel anything?" Evie asked anxiously.

"Not a thing."

I stuck the twelve hundreds into my pocket, as if they were sticks of chewing gum.

We both took a final look at the cat and then went downstairs into the casino pit to gamble.

"Let's go to the ten-dollar-minimum table," Evie suggested.

"Why don't you play with me?" I asked, suddenly frightened.

"No, you performed the ceremony, not I."

Ceremony? What ceremony? I rubbed a feline. Was everyone going mad . . . including myself?

There was one other player at the ten-dollar table we selected. The dealer was a young, heavyset, red-haired woman who greeted me in a friendly manner. I peeled off one of the hundred-dollar bills and handed it to her. She seemed to chastise me for the attempt at direct physical contact—touch—and gestured that I should just lay the bill down and withdraw my hand. Then she pushed the chips across the table to me.

"Remember," Evie whispered in my ear, "you're playing the dealer and not the deck."

"What? What do you mean I'm playing the dealer, not—"

"Never mind, Alice. Just do what I told you."

"How much should I bet?"

"One ten-dollar chip each hand."

So I put out one chip. The dealer dealt.

I lost the first five hands. Then I won. Then I lost the next six.

I took out another hundred-dollar bill and got ten more chips. "Evie," I whispered ironically, "maybe I'd better go through that ceremony again."

She said nothing. I piled the new chips in front of me and started to play again.

I won that hand. And then the next one. And on the third hand I hit the jackpot with 21 points—the ace of clubs and the queen of hearts.

I began to laugh. There was sweat on my brow. I suddenly felt very unfettered . . . happy. It was like the best glass of wine in the world, the best afternoon at the movies, the best weekend in the country with the nicest man you knew. I felt intimate with everyone at the table. I felt that I loved them and they loved me.

I won again. I kept taking crazier and crazier chances on the cards—in spite of Evie's feverish warnings and groans.

Soon, my ten chips had grown to thirty.

I pushed all thirty into the betting area.

"Lord, girl, what are you doing!" I heard Evie squeak.

"I'm betting three hundred dollars. Isn't that allowed?"

"Of course it's allowed," she said. "It's just not too bright."

"Oh, Evie, don't worry."

I was dealt a ten and a three. I hit. A seven. I stood at twenty, obviously. The dealer "broke" her hand. I won!

Then they changed dealers.

"They often do that when a customer is hot," Evie whispered.

With the new dealer, a dour-looking bald man, I lost the first two. Then I won an incredible sixteen straight hands. I was, as they say, on a roll. I felt like a dancer . . . like an athlete . . . nothing could stop me . . . the music was playing and I was perfectly in synch. They brought me drinks. I drank. They suggested I go to another table with a higher minimum bet. I went.

In thirty minutes I had six thousand dollars.

And then, suddenly, the bubble burst.

No, I didn't begin to lose. I had just had it. The thought of playing another hand was profoundly distasteful to me.

I turned to Evie and said: "No more."

She nodded. She gathered the chips in a

large handkerchief. She helped me up because I was very unsteady. We walked to the cashier together and cashed in the chips. Then into the bar.

The moment we sat down Evie said: "You better not play anymore here. After all, you're an employee. They don't like employees playing and winning."

"I'm not an employee. I'm an actress. I'm on a per diem basically. A short-term contract."

Then I laid my head in my hands, as if I were ill. But I wasn't.

"Do you want something, Alice? Coffee?"

I didn't answer. I felt very strange. Exhausted but light-headed. When I looked up Evie was very grim faced. Her arms were folded.

"What are you thinking?" I asked.

"Nothing. I am in shock. That's a lot of money you just won."

I sat up straight. "Why are *you* in shock? You told me you believed all that cat nonsense before we played. *I* should be the one in shock."

"That is correct."

"But one test does not make it true."

"I suppose so."

I laughed out loud, a bit crazily. Evie looked very concerned. I reached across the table and patted her hand. "Oh don't worry about me. It's just that I am amused by my own deviousness. No, one test doesn't determine truth. But I damn well believe that cat is magical. I damn well believe that every time I stroke beautiful Harlow eleven times I am going to win."

I gestured for her to come closer.

"And there's something else I know for sure now. That Adele was Cleopatra. And she was murdered for her cat. But the prize escaped. and whoever killed Adele came back again the next night and rifled the rooms. But the cat was not there then, either. Because dear sweet little acrobatic Harlow knows who her friends are in this world."

"What are you going to do?" she asked.

"Catch a killer," I said quickly. Then I added, "If you will help me."

"Me? What do I know about catching a killer?"

"Evie, I believe you know just about everything."

"But I have to go home. Back to Philadelphia."

"Can't you take a few days vacation? In a glorious casino suite, courtesy of Madame Harlow." I held up the massive role of hundreds that Harlow had won for us.

"Why not?" Evie commented. "I'm a lady of leisure now."

"And don't you think, Evie, that two nutritionally conscious women like us should occasionally indulge in rare prime ribs?"

"You mean before we catch a killer?"

"Yes. Before."

"Only if the platter includes a baked potato."

"It most certainly does."

"Would it be too wicked to have butter *and* sour cream?" she asked.

Chapter 8

"Isn't it a little late for you to be still around?" I commented. Art Agee had suddenly materialized in the coffee shop where I was waiting for Evie, who was changing into the new dress we'd bought at one of the hotel shops.

He looked at his watch. "Not a little late. A lot late. I've had a lot to do around here lately. It's nearly midnight. I'm usually home by eleven."

He looked around nervously. "It seems everyone is keeping late hours," he said, pointing to two women at a nearby table.

I looked over their way. They were strangely familiar. And then I realized the duo was the grieving friends—Bliss and Joan, the last two of the quartet of girlhood friends whose annual reunion had turned into a nightmare.

They were wearing those ultra-dark glasses again. There was a nearly empty bottle of good red wine on the table. What was this act all about—were their eyes too red to be displayed in public? Others might have looked upon it as pure grief for a dead friend, and for the terrible trouble another friend had landed in. But I doubted it was that simple. Now I knew more. I knew that there was a very good chance they were not just mourning over their dead friend . . . but over the loss of their dead friend's fortune-making cat. It dawned on me how easy it would have been for either or both of them to have enticed Carmella to the room after murdering Adele.

"Have you found out anything?" Agee asked.

"I'm on the trail of something. It may be important. It may not. I'll let you know."

"I spoke to Carmella's lawyer," he said in a quiet but excited voice.

"Anything new?"

"Yes and no. First of all the lawyer told me that Carmella repudiated the confession she made. She claims that she never remembers anything she does when she's manic."

"What *does* she remember?"

"Only getting a call from Adele, asking her to come to her room. She also remembers that Adele sounded drunk. She was singing what Carmella called the nonsense songs."

"The what?"

I heard Art laugh then, perhaps the first

time I'd ever heard him laugh. "The nonsense songs," he repeated. "She sang them for me once. Something like 'my sweet honey loves like a bunny.' Something like that. And another one: 'Berries, berries, berries for breakfast, tup tup—'"

"Tup tup tuppance for tea," I finished for him.

There was a look of absolute astonishment on his face.

"Yes," I said, pretty astonished myself, "this is quite weird, isn't it? We need to get a woman out of prison, and we sit here singing abysmally bad songs from one of the worst Broadway bombs in history."

"You're kidding! You *know* those songs?"

"By sheer accident, I assure you. I have a friend in New York, Tony, who is a fount of useless trivia. Especially things related to Broadway. He even owns the sheet music for that show—*Pie in Your Face,* which lasted for all of six performances. It purported to be a tribute to the old vaudeville days. That song about the bunny is called 'Every Honey Has Her Harry.'"

"Well, the doctors say sometimes the last things manic-depressives hear before they lose it will stay with them obsessively. Hard to believe the last thing Carmella heard or did before she—but that's impossible, anyway. Because I know she didn't do it."

Talking about Tony Basillio reminded me that I must call him.

"I have to go," Art said again, not moving a muscle. He looked weary. But in another minute, he did indeed go.

Just in time. Evie Soames was headed toward my table in that strange, springy walk that healthy old people have—as if their limbs are propelled in bursts by sheer will.

She sat down. She was laughing. "It is getting very exciting around here, young woman," she said.

"Did you make the call?" I asked.

"Yes. It's all set. The ad will appear in the morning edition of the *Record*. It hits the newsstand about five-thirty in the morning, the lady said. I paid with my credit card."

She pushed the piece of paper toward me. I read it for the umpteenth time.

YOUR MILLION-DOLLAR CAT

If your luck has turned bad, Kitty will change it. One session with this beautiful living charm will make you healthy, wealthy, and wise. She has made millions for others. Now it's your turn. Call between 6:30 and 8:00 A.M. for appointment.

Evie and I had worked on the text for at least an hour. It read good. A bit kooky. A bit rational. It was the kind of claim that is made every day in gambling towns, where people believe in lucky numbers and lucky dice and lucky planets and lucky T-shirts.

The poor gullible hopefuls would be intrigued by the ad. I felt like a cheap carnival tout enticing the "suckers" into the freak show tent.

Certainly the killer would be intrigued—whoever it was who murdered Adele for her cat. I looked over at Bliss and Joan's table. They had gone. I believed they were the murderers. But it could have been someone else. It could have been that dealer in the Castles, the young man who claimed that Cleopatra had been his friend. Maybe she was, but obviously he was hiding something, holding something back. Oh, the murderer could be any one of a hundred people Adele must have known and cultivated during her strange, bifurcated life—a successful Manhattan attorney and a casino legend in Atlantic City.

Then I heard something jingle. Evie was shaking the rental car keys in front of me.

"Then we're all set?" I asked.

"Yes. I have the car. I have the bag. I will knock on your door at six. We will smuggle Harlow out of the casino and into the car. You will go to rehearsal. I will stay by the phone on the boardwalk . . . which we listed in the ad. When the bad guy calls I will say that he or she can stroke poor Harlow in the marina at Harrah's Casino, on the other side of the island. Then I will pick you up and off we go."

She took a deep breath, laughed, and added: "That was a mouthful. I'm getting so interested in all this cloak-and-dagger stuff that I don't even feel like playing. But after all, I'm on vacation. Aren't I? I can do whatever I want to do."

I opened my purse, pulled out the immense wad of hundreds that I had won, and said, gleefully: "We sure can." And then I was immediately embarrassed by my childish display. I thrust the money back.

"Remember," I cautioned Evie, "when and if you get a call, the price for the consultation is five hundred dollars."

"Yes, I know you told me to do that, but why are you making it so expensive?"

"The more expensive, the better, Evie. Even crazed gamblers will balk at paying five hundred dollars to stroke a lucky cat. I'm betting that someone who doesn't bat an eyelid at that amount is someone who is planning to steal the cat."

Then Evie and I sauntered over to the bar to toast the success of our plot.

Fifteen minutes later I went to my room to call Tony Basillio and find out how Bushy and

Pancho and the gang were. The trouble was, the moment I sat down in front of the phone I couldn't remember where my cats were staying.

Were they with Basillio in my old apartment on 26th Street, where Basillio was now staying? Or had I left them in my new loft on Washington Street? To be fed and cared for by both my niece, Alison, and Tony?

Or, in fact, had I left them with Mrs. Oshrin, my neighbor on 26th Street?

Obviously, the pressure of the plot was getting to me. Or maybe my new facility with cards. Or maybe . . . I suddenly stared at the beautiful, lounging Harlow. I had a wild thought. If I stroked her some more I could go downstairs and win ten thousand dollars. And then if I stroked her some more I could go to another casino and win a hundred thousand dollars. I could win any amount I wanted. I could end my poverty and my friends' poverty. I could buy a damn theater. I could buy an island and a plane to get me there.

Whoa! Whoa, Alice! The prospect of money for nothing was awfully seductive. I had to rein myself in, remember that I was in this crazy town now, but not of it. I calmed down and dialed my loft on Washington Street. Tony was there. I had awakened him. Good!

"How's Bushy, how's Pancho?" I asked.

"Thriving," he said. "But it's one in the morning."

"So what?"

"So nothing, Swede. How are the rehearsals going?"

"Don't ask."

"Weathers is a madman?"

" 'Mad' doesn't even begin to describe him . . . or anything else going on here."

"What else is up?"

"I won seven thousand dollars, Tony."

"You what!?"

"Playing blackjack."

"I didn't know you could handle anything more dangerous than casino."

"I can't."

There was a long, nervous silence.

"Do you want me to come down there, Swede?"

"No, Tony. Not yet. But I may need you."

"I like to carry money, Swede."

"Well, I'll keep that in mind, Tony. But that's not what I need you for. There's another problem here."

"Let me guess. Somebody's been murdered."

"Good guess."

"Who was it?"

"A woman with a cat."

"*Marone!* I mighta knowed it."

"Yes indeed," I agreed just before I hung up the phone. Harlow was looking at me with big eyes. "Go to sleep," I told her. "Tomorrow you're going on the road."

Chapter 9

Oh what a disaster that rehearsal was the next morning!

Carlos Weathers was getting crazier and crazier. As for Gordon Seaver, well, he was moaning that there seemed to be absolutely no notices or advertising about our coming Valentine's Day performances, even in the casino proper, even in the bar where we were going to perform. And me, well, to be honest, my mind was on other things—like poor little Harlow stuck in a bag on the back seat of the rented car, and poor freezing Evie Soames, waiting out in the cold for a phone call in response to the ad.

Then, at about six-thirty in the morning, when both Weathers and Seaver seemed to be finally approaching some kind of functional ability—Carlos Weathers dropped a container of coffee on Gordon's shoes.

Then Carlos said to me: "Princess, would you get me another coffee?"

I was so astonished by his arrogance—by the ease with which he made me into a gofer, as if I were nineteen years old again—that I just walked out of the theater, purchased three containers of coffee and brought them back.

Weathers then began to lecture Gordon Seaver and me on the two main characters in *Sweet Bird of Youth*. He said: "What we have here, believe it or not, is junkie love. These two people are addicts. They are lovers. They loathe each other and themselves. It is, in fact, the classical love story."

He was so stupid I almost pitied him. Almost.

Then I saw Evie, standing ramrod straight just inside the door of the theater. She was making a funny motion with her hand. It could mean only one thing: a call had come in . . . an appointment had been made. Contact!

"Ohhhh," I groaned hideously.

Gordon and Weathers turned to me, startled.

I bellowed again.

"What is it?" Weathers asked, alarmed.

"Sorry, but suddenly I feel terribly nauseous. I think I'd better excuse myself for a while."

Weathers looked at me with scorn. Theater

people don't get nauseous, he seemed to be silently accusing.

"Well, go back to your room, damn it . . . and take something," Gordon said, as if afraid I was about to do something untoward in the theater.

I hurried out of the theater—and out of the casino.

It was a sunny, cold morning. I climbed into the rented car. Evie gave me my coat. I could see that Harlow had extricated herself from the carry bag (it wasn't a cat carrier, just a duffel) and was lounging happily on the back window, staring at the sky.

We drove off. Evie drove very erect, very slowly, very carefully.

"Who called, Evie? Was it a man or a woman?" I asked.

"A woman. She first asked if this was the number of the ad in the paper. Then she said her luck was very bad and she wanted to stroke the cat. I told her it would cost five hundred."

"What happened?"

"She didn't skip a beat. She asked where she could meet with you and when."

"Could you tell anything from the voice?"

"No."

We were making the turn on the island, along the inlet. The inlet joined a bay. And at the bay front was an enormous solitary casino—Harrah's.

On the near side of the casino was a marina, now empty because it was midwinter, and alongside the dock slips was a concrete walkway.

Evie parked the car at the foot of the walkway. She adjusted her hat in the mirror. I went into the back of the car and got Harlow into the bag. "Maybe," Evie said, in an old voice, "we ought to forget about this and go back to the hotel casino and get some tea and toast."

"Are you getting cold feet on me?"

"It's not cold feet, it's a chill in the heart. And I'm not afraid for me, I'm afraid for you."

I sat back on the seat, holding a re-bagged Harlow in my lap.

"Why don't we go back and play the machines? I really like you, Alice, and I fear for you."

"There is little to fear."

"No, there is a lot to fear. What if this woman has a gun? What if she was the one who murdered before? Why wouldn't she kill you also? If the cat can win millions for her . . . what's another body to her?"

"Well, Evie, you just keep watch. From the car. If something happens, get help."

The old lady chuckled. I reached forward and squeezed her shoulder affectionately. It was very bony. I liked her very much. But she had frightened me. More than that, she had kind of sobered me. I stared out at the empty marina. Yes, this whole scheme had been put together on an instant's notice, while I was high from my gambling triumph. The whole thing was primitive, almost goofy. Yes, *goofy* is the word that best described it. Putting ads in newspapers, phone booths out on the freezing boardwalk—goofy and primitive!

And Evie was right about the danger. Did I really believe I was trapping a killer . . . and if I did, why hadn't I taken any precautions? I didn't even have a hatpin.

"Look! There!" Evie called out.

I started to climb out. "Wait!" Evie shouted.

"What?"

"Suppose the caller had nothing to do with the killings. Suppose she just wants to stroke the cat for luck, like it says in the ad?"

"Well, it'll cost her five hundred dollars. But she'll get what she's paying for . . . that is, if Harlow doesn't object."

And then, of course, I'll have to give the money back, I thought. I couldn't possibly take five hundred dollars from some desperate woman who's probably blown her family's nest egg and is trying to make it back quickly before her husband finds out.

I walked toward the figure that Evie had

spotted on the walkway. It was a woman. She had a purse on her shoulder and her hands in her pockets. She watched me closely as I walked toward her. I couldn't make out her face very well, but at least I could see that she was neither Bliss Revere nor Joan Secunda. I had never seen her before in my life. She was a young woman, in her twenties.

When I was about five feet away I stopped.

"Hello," I said pleasantly when I was upon her.

She smiled in greeting. "Were you the person who put the ad in the paper about the lucky cat?" she asked. Her voice was modulated and refined.

"Yes."

"And you mentioned five hundred dollars on the phone to get access to the cat."

"Yes. That is the fee."

"Fine," she said, "but may I look at the animal first?"

"Of course," I said, placing the bag on the ground, opening it, and letting Harlow peer out. The stranger stared at her.

"A beautiful cat," she noted. Then she reached into her pocket. I thought she would pull out the money.

Instead, she extracted a small leather case and flipped it open, saying: "I'm an enforcement officer with the Atlantic County Board of Health. You are going to receive a summons under Statute Number Twenty-eight, which prohibits you from the commercial exploitation of domestic pets."

Then, right there, without saying another word, under the thoughtful eyes of Harlow, she wrote me a summons for a hundred and fifty dollars, payable by mail or in person within thirty days. She handed me the slip of paper. I took it.

"You're getting off very easy, Miss," she said. "If I'd actually paid you for this—if I'd actually decided to let the money change hands—you'd be in big trouble. I could have had you arrested. If I were you, I'd take a lesson from this and stop this kind of behavior."

Then she walked off. I wandered back to the car and climbed in.

"What happened, Alice? What happened?"

I couldn't talk. I handed Evie the summons. She read it and burst into laughter. I slumped down in the front seat.

"We're just not cut out to be Ma Barker and Daughter, young lady. That's all there is to it."

I wished Evie would stop calling me "young lady" and "young woman," but she was right about our ineptitude as scam artists.

"Let's get some breakfast," I said.

"In town or back at the Monte Carlo?"

"Whatever."

"Let's go back to the casino. It's high time I

started charging things to my room. It's one of the pleasures of hotel living. I'll park the car in the garage. Then we can eat. We'll return the car to the rental place later."

We drove back to the casino garage. There was an elevator from the garage level to my floor. I zoomed up with Harlow and dumped her in the room. Then I zoomed back down to the garage again to pick up Evie.

"Did I leave that bloody summons in the car?" I asked her. We were halfway between the car and the exit.

She looked in her pockets. "Well, I don't have it."

I hesitated. Should I go back to the car? How hungry was I? Well, I had to get the summons. It was the badge of my absurdity. A medal.

"One second," I said to Evie and hurried back to the car.

Something was odd. I stopped. I squinted because there was little light in the underground garage.

"Evie!" I called.

She came close. "Look there, Evie. What do you see?"

She approached the back of the car. "Something's leaking. Oil maybe."

I bent down and touched the garage floor . . . a concrete floor. I stood up and looked at my hand. Then I showed it to Evie.

"Oh Lord, honey. That's blood."

She rummaged in her purse for the keys. Finally she located the one for the trunk.

I bent and opened it.

Art Agee was lying there, on his side, peacefully, as if sleeping.

There was a bullet hole in his eye, no doubt the cause of that darkening pool on the ground.

Sleeping. Not like the last time I'd seen him. Untroubled.

But of course that made no sense. Why would he be sleeping in our car trunk? That would be a pretty damn eccentric thing to do. And Art had not struck me as that kind of man. No, of course he wasn't sleeping.

Chapter 10

"My name is Detective Baretta," the burly man said.

"Are you—" I started.

"No, I didn't star in a TV series. I don't fracture the English language. And I don't have a white parrot."

"I wasn't going to ask any of that. I was going to ask you if you were at the crime scene of the Adele Houghton murder."

"Yes, I was."

"I thought so."

"You were the woman who discovered the body?"

"Yes."

"This seems to be a hobby of yours."

"Correct. I discover maybe four or five bodies a week when I'm back in Manhattan."

"I think you're putting me on," he said.

"And I think you are *the* Baretta—white parrot or no."

The interrogation was taking place in a

glass-enclosed waiting room in the underground garage, though, thankfully, Detective
Baretta did not truly seem to suspect me of
any wrongdoing.

Evie was standing outside the booth, keeping an eye on the proceedings, showing her
solidarity. I could also see the owner of the
casino and the security man, Charlie Lott. It
was just like the scene in Adele's room—police and EMS and flashbulbs in one incom-
prehensible stew. And, once again, the body
had been quickly removed and the whole
mess taken care of quietly—heaven forbid the
high-rolling, merry-making guests should be
troubled by a little thing like murder.

"Would you like some coffee?" Baretta
asked me.

"Nothing."

"When did you see Art Agee last?"

"Last night. Around midnight."

"Where?"

"In a coffee shop on the casino floor. I
mentioned to him that it was late. He said
he'd had a lot of work to do. We . . . chatted . . . briefly."

"What did you chat about?" he asked. He
leaned against the ledge that circled the
room.

"Old TV detectives," I said. And the moment I said it in that flip style I was sorry. I
stared at the detective. He seemed to be an

intelligent man. He looked like a dedicated cop. Why was I holding everything back? Why shouldn't I tell him at least part of the story?

"Art Agee had asked my help," I said.

"Help? With what?"

"He wanted me to find out who murdered Adele Houghton."

"But we already know that. She is in custody."

"He believed you had the wrong person in custody."

"Oh really? Why did he believe that?"

I merely shrugged. "He had his reasons, obviously." I couldn't tell him why. Art Agee was dead. At least I could protect his reputation. Let his wife bury him thinking he was faithful to the last.

"Do you have any idea who shot Mr. Agee?"

"No."

"Do you have any idea why he was killed?"

"No."

Detective Baretta slowly and extravagantly lit a cigarette, as if he could only have a certain number each day and he relished the ritual.

"You're here to perform as an actress, right?"

"Yes."

"Why would he ask an actress to investigate

a murder? Your name is Nestleton, right? Not Jessica Fletcher."

"Touché, Detective. I really am sorry about the Baretta crack. Forgive me. Mr. Agee asked me to look into the Adele Houghton murder because I've had some experience solving crimes—specifically murders—in the past. I'm not a detective, but I have worked with the police before. I have had paying clients."

"Did you know Art Agee before you were hired?"

"No."

"But you knew him quite well after you were hired?"

"What do you mean by that?"

"Were you lovers?"

"Of course not. He was a married man and I'm old enough to be his . . . old maid aunt—practically."

"A very attractive old maid," noted Detective Baretta. "Besides, Art Agee liked women, Miss Nestleton. All sorts of women. As long as they were beautiful."

"Am I supposed to consider that a compliment?"

"Yes."

He stood there, looking at me, for some time before speaking again. "Miss Nestleton, why don't we cut the crap here. You must have known that Art Agee was a heavy gambler."

"No, I didn't. I told you the truth, Detective. I never met Art Agee until the other day. But I thought employees of the casino weren't allowed to gamble."

"That's right. But he didn't gamble in the casino. He bet football games with a bookmaker. Football, basketball, cockroach races. Whatever. And he wasn't very good at it. He owed a lot of money."

"I see."

"So we know why he was killed. But we don't know by whom. And we may never find out, because when a big-time bookie murders one of his customers he tries to be very careful. It's not something they like to do anyway."

"I believe that he was murdered because he knew something about the Houghton murder."

"I don't think so," he said immediately.

"Well, I do, if that's all right with you," I retorted.

Baretta gave me a quizzical look. I wondered how much I should tell him about the cat . . . about the stroking . . . about Cleopatra and her entourage. How much? Nothing, for now. He'd say I was a lunatic.

"I'm confused," he said.

"What about, Detective Baretta?"

"You say Agee wanted you to find out something about the Adele Houghton murder. You were the one poking around in it. Yet he's the one to get iced. I don't get it. How come they didn't kill *you*?"

He was gently mocking me. I said nothing more. He walked out and Evie came in. "This is very bad," she said.

Then Charlie Lott came in with two containers of coffee. He handed one to me and one to Evie.

I blurted out: "Art Agee told me that if I ever was in trouble I could count on you."

His eyes filled with tears. "Yeah, Art was okay. I liked that kid. He treated me okay. From the very beginning. He tried to be a hotshot but he was just a nice kid."

Then the tears overflowed. Evie got so flustered she dropped her coffee. Just like Carlos Weathers had dropped his. Only Charlie Lott was here this time, and he caught the container before it hit the ground. It was a wonderful performance by a middle-aged man and Evie clapped as he delivered it up.

But Charlie was too upset for adulation. He shrugged, wiped his face with a bright handkerchief, and walked out.

Evie and I were alone. I didn't know what to say or do, so I started to pace.

"You think they've checked your room yet—Mr. Seaver and that other man—Rico or José or whatever his name is?" she asked solicitously.

"Carlos, you mean. I don't know, Evie," I

said wearily. "And frankly, I don't care at this point."

"Well, young woman, it can't get any worse this morning, so we might as well try and get that breakfast. Let's go to one of those places where the common folks eat. I feel like having a mess of bacon."

We walked out of there and up the stairs with arms linked.

There was a long line at the breakfast buffet but we were undaunted. This was a breakfast we had to have. By the time we finally reached the serving line, Evie was in high dudgeon. "Look at those eggs, would you! Wouldn't you think these people would know how to scramble eggs? And look at that soppy bacon. Bacon should be crisp. Crisp!" She intimidated the servers so badly that I sent her to find a table, promising that I would bring the food.

I loaded up on French toast with sausages, juice, coffee, and one side order of very straggly home fried potatoes. Evie was right. Why couldn't a multimillion-dollar operation like the Monte Carlo provide a simple good breakfast? The simple things seemed to escape them.

I got the two overloaded trays safely to the table.

"Maybe we ought to say grace," Evie said.

"I don't think so," I said. "Let's save it for a

better meal." But my cynicism had obviously offended her, so I waited patiently while she bowed her head and whispered a few humble words. We waded into the French toast after applying butter and syrup liberally. The coffee was hot but extremely thin.

I was about to eat my sixth forkful of French toast when I noticed the two grieving witches.

Joan and Bliss were seated only three tables away, huddled together as usual, their sunglasses in place. I had walked right by them from the buffet table without even noticing them.

"What are you looking at?" Evie said.

"It's those two women again."

"Which women?" she asked, too polite to turn around and stare.

"The friends of the deceased," I said and then smiled ruefully at that clichéd phrase.

Oh, I knew about the picture they had tried to paint of the undying friendship among the quartet of school friends. But I didn't buy it. I felt that the threads of that friendship were all twisted. I didn't think the secret hatred Carmella was supposed to have harbored for Adele Houghton was the only vituperative element in that group.

These two, in particular, were suspect, somehow evil. And not just because they were the survivors of an event that had decimated the other half of the quartet. But I couldn't say why I mistrusted them. I didn't have a handle on that yet. I just knew that I didn't believe they were unaware that Adele had been the legendary gambler Cleopatra. Just as I could not believe that the murders of Art and Adele were not related.

I definitely didn't want any more French toast.

"Evie, what was the name of that young blackjack dealer in Castles?"

"Lyle Sweet."

"Was that it? No—not Sweet, Sweetnum."

Was it possible, I thought, that Lyle knew Adele's friends? Anything was possible. I tried to remember if I had seen Art Agee speak to the two women. Or if I had heard him mention Lyle's name, or vice versa.

I looked down at my hands. They were trembling. Poor Art Agee. I had let him down. I knew it wasn't my fault he was dead. It wasn't as if he'd hired me to protect him. But . . . but he'd been my client, so to speak . . . and I had let him get killed.

I didn't voice any of this to Evie, who was picking through her mountainous meal. Thank heaven I'd met up with her. And thank heaven for the hum of the casino—that white noise kind of ambience. It was oddly soothing.

I wondered what I'd be thinking and doing

now, after my brilliant trap had so ludicrously exploded, if Art Agee had not been murdered. I wondered what my next step would have been.

Would I have continued the investigation? Of course. That was the deal that insured Harlow's safety.

I knew what I would be doing. I would be searching for the secret apartment that the dealer mentioned—Adele's Atlantic City apartment, which must have been Harlow's home.

I looked at Evie. She appeared to be very tired. God, I was a blockhead! Certainly she was tired. She was an old woman and had probably had more adventure than her system could take. I would make sure she took a long nap when I got her back to her room. And I'd have room service deliver a sumptuous lunch.

I was half Evie's age, but I was tired, too. As soon as we refreshed ourselves, we had to get started on the next part of the investigation.

I knew what I had to do. Get Basillio down to Atlantic City. And then find that mysterious apartment. Find it and search it.

Chapter 11

It was late afternoon. Evie and Harlow and I sat gloomily in my suite, watching the shadows progress. We were waiting for Tony Basilio, who was on his way. The buses from Port Authority Terminal in Manhattan left every hour on the hour, he said. I had a sudden image of cattle—passive guernseys—being herded onto truck beds. Lambs to the slaughter. Only these passengers were coming to Atlantic City, where they'd stand transfixed, hour after hour, in front of the slot machines and the video poker setups, hoping against hope that luck would grant to them what it granted to so few others: the jackpot, the once in a lifetime score.

No doubt about it, this whole trip had gone sour for me. I was no longer thrilled about the money I'd won, only a little embarrassed. Every time I looked at pretty little Harlow now, I saw the slashed body of her dead mistress and heard the insane cackling of Carmella Koteit as she stood in the doorway. I knew how lucky I had been in meeting Evie, but every time I looked at her now I saw her standing in the car park downstairs, saying, "Oh Lord, honey. That's blood." And then the gruesome bulk of Art Agee in the car trunk.

So the fun was definitely over. The dilettantism was like a distant echo.

We were suffering.

Particularly Evie. She kept repeating: "Why did they put that poor young man in our rented car?"

Even Harlow looked morose and had stopped preening. In addition, three different cans of cat food—one tuna, one chicken, and one a very odiferous kidney stew—had failed to interest her.

When the knock came at the door I fairly leaped off the chair and ran to open it.

Then I stepped back, horrified, waving frantically to Evie to hide the cat.

It wasn't Tony Basillio.

It was a handsome woman wearing a stunning banker's-type suit with a white ruffled shirt. She looked like one of those successful women executives in a *Cosmo* interview.

"Why are you staring at me like that?" she asked angrily. "Don't you know who I am?"

Oh! Yes, I did. It was Joan Secunda, the one who ran a successful chain of diet clinics. I hadn't recognized her because she wasn't wearing those ubiquitous dark glasses. By this time, she looked more natural, was more recognizable, with them than without them.

I stepped into the hallway and closed the door behind me, safeguarding Harlow.

"We are getting very tired of you," she said angrily.

I stared at her. "What are you talking about?"

"Don't give me that innocent act. You're wandering around making all kinds of accusations about Adele. you're spinning all kinds of ugly stories about her."

"How do you know?" I asked.

"What does it matter how I know? I'm asking you to stop. The woman is dead. Isn't that enough for you?"

"What precisely are you accusing me of saying about her?"

She grew silent. She kept staring at me as if trying to understand my perfidy.

To be honest, I was putting on a bit of an act. I knew very well what she was talking about . . . about Adele as Cleopatra. But who had told her this? Who? The dealer in Castles? Art? Who? Besides, since she was one of my prime murder suspects, wasn't this a smoke screen? Hadn't she known about Adele all along?

"You did hear about Art Agee?" I asked.

"Who is Art Agee?"

"The young man who was murdered."

"Yes, I heard about that horrible thing. But only horrible things happen in this horrible, ridiculous place."

"Are you sure you didn't know him?"

"Why should I know him?"

"He was your friend's lover."

"Are you insane? Which friend?"

"He was Carmella's lover."

She threw back her head and laughed as if I had said the most outlandish thing in the world. Then she said, "Right. And B.B. King is my lover."

For a moment I didn't get the reference; then I recalled that the four friends had originally met in college around their love for the blues.

"I'm telling you the truth," I said softly.

"Truth?" she screamed. "Truth! You wander around poking your nose into things. Breaking into people's room and going through their things. You libel the dead. Who the hell are you? What are you after?"

She was so incensed that I thought she was going to strike me.

"Now, now, ladies," a soft voice intruded from behind us.

We both turned.

"Tony!"

I hadn't seen him approach.

"I heard you people screaming at each other the minute I got out of the elevator."

"We're just having a discussion," I said lamely.

Joan Secunda walked away. She turned once and gave me a strange look of warning, I suppose, or of threat . . . to mend my ways.

"What was that all about?" Tony asked.

I didn't reply. We embraced almost wildly. I had never been so glad to see him.

Once in the suite, I introduced him to Evie. They shook hands stiffly.

Tony saw Harlow on the bed. "What the hell is this?"

"This is Harlow."

"Who does she belong to?"

"There's a story in that, Tony."

"I assume you got me down here to tell me a story. Okay. Start telling, Swede." He stationed himself by the window and stared out at the ocean, signaling that he was all ears.

I spoke very slowly and succinctly. I told him everything: from rescuing the cat to finding the slashed body of Adele Houghton; from Art Agee's request for help to the rehearsal blow-up, which led me to Evie; from the legend of Cleopatra to the break-in of the rooms of the murder victim and her friends; from the finding of the wig and the chips in the safe-deposit box to the interview of the young dealer in Castles.

I explained how I won seven thousand dollars . . . about the goofy trap I had laid and its even goofier denouement. I told him about the murder of Art Agee. I told him I was now ready to begin a search for Cleopatra/Adele's secret apartment. I told him, in other words, everything I could remember.

From time to time during the recounting I would look at Evie for help and support; she kept giving me little "amens."

When I was finished I heaved a sigh of relief and waited for Basillio's response.

But Tony said nothing. He kept staring out the window.

"Well?" I repeated impatiently.

He turned and smiled. "Do you think I'm dressed appropriately for the casino?"

I exploded. "What kind of stupid question is that, Tony? I just told you about two murders!"

"I just thought it would be important to dress correctly."

I caught hold of myself. I calmed down. He was wearing green corduroy pants, a white sweatshirt, a leather bomber jacket, a checked wool muffler, and boots.

"You look just like a middle-aged, permanently out-of-work stage designer is supposed to look," I said sweetly. And Evie amen-ed that, too.

"Thank you," Tony said. "I agree. Now let me deal with your problems."

"Please do," I said grimly.

"I want to make sure I heard everything correctly. First of all, you found a dead woman. The police arrested her friend. The motive was that the suspect blamed the victim for the death of her daughter. Two more friends agreed on the motive. Do I have that right?"

"Correct."

"And the second murder. A marketing manager is shot to death gangland style and stuffed into your trunk. The cops say he owed a lot of money to bookmakers. That's why he was murdered, they say. Do I have that correct?"

"Yes."

"And what you are saying is that the woman was murdered because she was in reality a legendary gambler who had a magic cat that insured she would always win."

"Yes."

"And that the young man stuffed into your trunk was also murdered because he had some connection with this Cleopatra and her magic cat."

"Yes."

"And you are also saying that this creature on the bed is that magical cat—Cleopatra's cat."

"Yes."

"And that you won seven thousand gambling at blackjack, a game you never played before in your life, because you stroked the cat eleven times."

"Right. Evie will testify to that. She taught me the game. She saw me stroke the cat. She was at the table when I won."

Tony smiled at me. He walked over and kissed me on the head.

Evie smiled indulgently. Her manner with Basillio had been fairly chilly, but, I thought, perhaps she's warming to him a little now.

Tony strolled over to the bed and smiled at Harlow. Then he sauntered back to the window.

From there, he said: "Here's what I think. I think that after many years of struggling in the New York theater . . . after many years of trying to make a living as a cat sitter, as an actress, as God knows what . . . I think you have gone around the bend." He folded his arms.

"Is that so?"

"That is so, my dear. And, if you have maintained your Blue Cross/Blue Shield policy, I would suggest a brief but intensive stay in any kind of accredited psychiatric facility."

"And I would suggest for you a fifteen-story leap out of that window," I said.

"I think we're on the sixteenth floor," Evie

said mildly. "All the same, I don't think you young people should fight."

"Who's fighting?" Tony protested.

I turned toward Evie and said to her: "This poor fool of a man is just too dense to understand the power of a feline. I suggest we allow him to partake of it."

"An excellent idea, young woman," she said.

I turned back to Tony. "Well, are you willing to put your stupidity to the test, Tony?"

"I don't have any money to gamble," he said.

"But I do. I have lots of money." I pulled out the roll of hundreds I had won.

"Alice, get serious. No damn cat will insure winning at a blackjack table. You may have won once, and you may win twice . . . but there's no such thing as beating blackjack. Do you understand?"

"Scared to play a little, Tony?"

"Okay. Let's get this nonsense over with. Let's just do it and get it over."

I put the roll back into my bag.

"What's your game, Tony?"

"I like anything: craps . . . roulette . . . blackjack."

I looked toward Evie, who said, "I think we should stick to blackjack. It would be a better test. Because Harlow has already helped you win there. It will show your young man that in some cases lightning strikes twice in the same place."

"Blackjack it is," said Tony. And there was a smirk on his face so wide that I felt like smacking him. But I consoled myself by knowing that he was heading for a fall . . . a long, steep, shameful fall. His smug little assumptions were about to be smashed.

"What do I do?" he asked.

I took a deep breath. "You go to Harlow and you stroke her eleven times. Then we go down to the casino."

"I think," Evie interjected, "we ought not go to the one downstairs."

"Back to Castles then?" I asked.

"Uh-uh. I think we should try a totally new place . . . that none of us have ever been to."

"Sounds logical," I replied.

"Let's try Surf World," she suggested. "It's right off the boardwalk about a hundred yards from the Monte Carlo."

"Good. You got that, Tony? We all go to Surf World. We enter together. We play together. We each start with a thousand of my money. What table do we go to, Evie?"

"I suggest the ten-dollar table."

"Fine. Do you understand, Tony? We'll all play together but you alone will have stroked the cat."

"I'm ready," he said, throwing his arms out. "After all, I've always been a gambling man."

"Okay. Stroke, Basillio!"

"Eleven times, right?"

"Why not? It worked before and we're trying to reproduce an experiment."

Tony laughed. "By the way, if I prove that you are wrong . . . that you are in a feline fantasy world vis-à-vis games of chance, my dear . . . what do I get?"

"I'll let you visit me in the psychiatric facility."

"A done deal."

He walked to the bed and sat down.

"Wait, Tony. Let me outline your obligations if I—when I'm proven right."

He grinned and waited. I had a sudden chill. It dawned on me that Tony looked very much like an older, darker complexioned Lyle Sweetnum, the blackjack dealer in Castles. He'd said he had heard that Cleopatra was dead. But how had he heard? Who had told him? Who knew? There were no newspaper reports. Yes, I thought, that young man must be the first one to contact when we try to find Adele's apartment.

"I'm listening," said a sarcastic Tony.

"If you do win big tonight, Tony, you will not gamble anymore until you have helped me clear up this mess. Is that understood?"

"Of course, my dear. You are my guide through the dark and dangerous world of magic and enchantment. You are my high priestess of voodoo. I am your slave. I realize that if I counter your wishes you can say the magic words and I will be instantly transformed into a polka-dotted rodent."

"Shut up, Tony, and stroke Harlow."

"Gladly."

He reached over and Harlow struck, lashing out with her right paw and catching Tony on the top of his left hand.

He started yowling and hopping around the room. Harlow just sat there placidly.

"She attacked me! That crazy animal attacked me!" he yelled, waving his wounded hand in the air.

"Calm down, Basillio. Let me see."

He thrust the offended limb at me. I looked. Harlow was something! There were two no-nonsense punctures, and enough blood to unhinge Tony.

"Evie, can you get me something from the bathroom? Something to press on it."

To Tony I said: "You can't blame her for striking, Tony. You approached her too aggressively. She's a very high-class lady and you have this low-rent behavior."

Evie came back with a damp washcloth. I pressed it to his hand. The bleeding stopped.

"Are you ready to try again?" I asked.

"Yes."

"Now let's do it this way. I'll sit down on the bed first, Tony, and talk to Harlow. Then you join me and while I'm reasoning with her you stroke her eleven times. But do it very gently. You're not whacking a ball, you're stroking a cat. Use some wit. Turn on the famous Basillio charm."

Tony grimaced. I sat down. I talked to Harlow. I told her that I understood the reason for the attack on Tony and she was perfectly within her rights. Tony, frightened but determined, stroked her lovely back eleven times.

Chapter 12

It was nine P.M. Tony, Evie, and I sat in a comfortable open bar not unlike the performance space in the Monte Carlo. But we were in the casino called Surf World. It was a cozy, more modest version of the Monte Carlo and Castles, sandwiched in between two other giant gambling dens.

We had ordered hamburgers and drinks. We were getting ready for the blackjack tables. There was a young singer on the bandstand singing popular songs with a good trio backing her up.

"I heard this place has entertainment in their bars twenty-four hours a day. Young singers on the way up. Big singers on the way down. They pay them peanuts but the children are happy to perform."

"You know a lot about casinos, Evie," Tony said, in a playfully accusatory voice. "I think you have some deep dark secrets in your past."

Evie laughed deliciously and replied: "If you must know, young man, I confess I was once a hootchy-kootchy dancer."

"Shame on you," Tony said.

The singer was doing a Nina Simone medley. She was very pretty and had a delivery like Peggy Lee's.

A waitress in a severely cut down outfit delivered the hamburgers.

"Put your eyes back into your head," I cautioned Tony.

Tony looked as if someone had just thrown on the light switch and caught him with a hammer poised over the piggy bank. "My mind is not on beautiful young women now, Swede. My mind is on the magic powers flowing through me. I feel the claws of luck grasping my throat. I feel the power of the voodoo cat . . ." He paused. "What the hell is her name?" And then he broke up laughing.

"Eat your hamburger, Tony. It's almost time to play. I want all of us well fed."

We ate very slowly. The joking, the laughter, seemed to have totally vanished.

Tensely, carefully, I opened my purse and gave Tony ten one-hundred-dollar bills. Then ten to Evie. And ten to myself. One thousand dollars each.

Tony ordered a brandy after the burger. I had coffee. Evie had tea and a Grand Marnier.

"How do we do it, Evie?" I asked my guru.

"Well, I think we should all go to the same table. But not at one time. We don't want them to think we're working as a team."

"We're not," I protested.

"I know, but these people are mighty suspicious. They don't like groups of any kind . . . even friends. They prefer solitary players."

"So then we'll do it that way. I'll go to the table first. Then Tony goes to the other end. And then you go between us."

I tipped the waitress outrageously, sent ten dollars over to the young singer, and stood up.

I walked to the designated table, plopped down a hundred-dollar bill, and got ten chips. Then I put another hundred down, and got ten more.

I played two hands and lost.

Then Tony arrived. He purchased three hundred dollars' worth of chips.

He won his first two hands.

Then Evie arrived and got chips.

Soon a stranger arrived and then another and soon the table was full, five players. It was theater at its best.

The dealer was a young Asian girl whose nameplate read Leigh Han.

Once the table was full I began to lose steadily. I had expected that; after all, I hadn't stroked Harlow this night; Tony had.

I could see that Evie was doing a bit better, but not much.

One of the strangers was winning. As for Tony, he seemed just to be holding his own . . . winning one and then losing one.

When I lost all my chips I didn't buy any more. I just stepped back and watched. Evie was playing so conservatively it didn't really matter. The stranger who was winning started to lose and soon both of the strangers left.

The only ones left playing were Evie and Tony.

Then Tony announced he was going to play three hands at one time because he was lonely with only one other player left—Evie. This way, he announced to the dealer, we can imagine there are five players again. Since it was perfectly legal to play up to three hands, the dealer could only smile.

Tony looked at me and grinned. I turned my head away . . . didn't the fool know we were supposed to be strangers?

Tony doubled his bets on each of the three hands. He won two out of three. Then he doubled his bets on the two winning hands. I could tell that the dealer was beginning to get nervous.

Tony won all three hands and then doubled his bets.

The pit boss came over, casually, and checked the situation out.

On the next hand Tony got blackjack on two out of three hands and on the third hand he still beat the dealer.

Since blackjack is paid off at 3:2, Tony won a lot.

Then he doubled all his bets the next hand. No one moved. They just stared at the chips.

I looked at Tony. He was beginning to look totally out of control . . . licking his lips . . . moving his shoulders . . . with a kind of gleeful rush in his eyes like he was a dope addict who was being fed intravenously.

Tony won nine straight hands! Then the pit boss changed dealers. It was a way to slow the action. Tony stared glumly at his enormous pile of chips. The new dealer, a tall, thin man whose card read Thomas Web, performed a dazzling shuffling ritual.

Evie decided to stop playing. We all stared at the table as the cards were cut.

"What's the limit?" Tony asked the dealer.

"At this table, six hundred a hand."

"Good enough," Tony said. He peeled off his remaining hundred-dollar bills, combined it with his winnings, and bet the limit on each of his three hands.

He won all three. He laughed crazily. He picked up his chips and moved to the fifty-dollar-minimum-limit table. There was only one other player there. Evie and I followed at a distance.

The limit at the fifty-dollar table was nine hundred per hand.

Tony played two hands. Nine hundred on each. He won one and hit blackjack on the other.

He gathered his chips and walked to the hundred-dollar table.

He won eleven thousand dollars in about thirty seconds, winning seven out of eight hands.

But he wasn't going to stop. Evie walked close to me. "You better get control of your young man," she said. And, indeed, Basillio was out of control . . . he was on a roll . . . a rush of winning. He looked like a madman.

I walked close to him and kicked him hard on the shin. He screamed. I apologized. Then I walked out of the casino and onto the boardwalk.

Evie followed. We huddled and waited.

Tony came out five minutes later—holding the money he had gotten from cashing the chips.

Tony was delirious. He did a crazy victory dance. He whooped. He danced around us. He kept kissing us. The cold meant nothing to him. The wind meant nothing.

Finally, he modulated, slowly, in sections.

He put one arm around me. He kept shaking his head.

"Well, young man?" Evie said.

"I don't know what happened. Suddenly I was winning. Suddenly I felt like I would not lose . . . could not lose. I felt that I would never lose."

"That was the feeling I experienced also," I noted.

"What do I do with the money?"

"Hold onto it for a while. We have other things to think of, don't we, Tony?"

"How could this thing be true, Swede?"

"What?"

"How could stroking a stupid cat eleven times turn me into a winner? It is the craziest thing I have ever heard of."

I wasn't interested in his awe. "Listen," I said to both Evie and Tony, "we'll meet in the lobby of the Monte Carlo at six in the morning. Both of you will come to rehearsal with me and then we'll pay a visit to Mr. Lyle Sweetnum, and begin our search for Cleopatra's apartment."

I looked at Evie. She nodded. I looked at Tony. He didn't seem to have heard me. I shook his arm. He nodded that he had indeed heard me. But he seemed in shock . . . in winner's shock . . . in voodoo shock . . . in Harlow shock.

"Let's synchronize watches," I said dramatically, and read the time off my watch. I realize that I had stolen a line from one of those old World War II commando movies I used to watch on television. The ones where Dana Andrews always paints his face black before going out on a commando raid. The one where he always says just before they leave, "Let's synchronize our watches."

We headed down the boardwalk toward our hotel. The wind was fierce. The cold was intense. It may not have qualified as a yellow brick road, but Tony, his hair flying in the wind, his eyes still glazed, looked positively leonine. And I have always been a denizen of Oz.

Chapter 13

Tony and I left our room at five forty-four in the morning and I knocked at Evie's door. She exited immediately. We took the elevator down and dug up three containers of coffee.

Gordon Seaver was already in the auditorium. He was dressed in a massive white wool turtleneck sweater, corduroy pants, and desert boots. Gordon had to be on the far side of sixty, but he was still strong of voice and strong shouldered. His face had developed neither the cracks nor the decay that one saw on so many celebrities of Gordon's sort. No, he still had it . . . whatever that was. Whatever it was that made women long for him thirty years ago, he still had it.

I introduced Tony and Evie to him.

"I want them to watch the rehearsal," I told him.

"It's Weathers's show, not mine," he said.

"I'll ask him when he gets here. Do you think he'll mind?"

Gordon snorted. "I think the boy king minds anything and everything. He makes a profession out of minding."

Evie was excited to meet him. She told him she had seen him years ago in one of the endless revivals of *South Pacific*. It was hard to believe she was really standing next to Gordon Seaver . . . Was this really him?

"It really is," Gordon declared. Then he struck a mock heroic pose and began to vocalize Ezio Pinza-style.

"In fact," he said, "I played in nine road productions of *South Pacific*. I played it so often and in so many geographical locales that I grew to loathe everything concerning the play. If I just heard someone mention an enchanted evening I would grow violently ill. And . . . ah . . . I don't want to go into it . . . you wouldn't believe me."

"You were wonderful," Evie gushed, ignoring the man's torment.

"Why, thank you. I was a bit younger then. My voice has thinned out."

Then his royal highness, the prince of drama theory, marched in. He was wearing one of his bizarre John Dillinger outfits and he carried long yellow pads on which were scribbled notes.

I introduced him to my friends and asked: "Would it be all right if they watched rehearsal?"

He looked as if I had broken some biblical commandment.

"They won't cause any difficulty," I said, laughing.

"I don't mean to insult their character," he said.

"Then what is your objection?" I asked, then added a little white lie: "They came all the way from New York just to see us work."

"The problem is balance."

"Balance?"

"Yes. They will rock the boat. It is inevitable."

"What boat?"

"Our boat. The raft."

"What raft?"

He took my arm and started to walk me about, as if he had to explain something delicate to a young child. "I look upon rehearsal as a very precarious raft. I feel we are out in a treacherous sea and that the only thing keeping the whole craft afloat is our concentration."

He paused, waiting for a response. I didn't know what the hell he was talking about.

"You see . . . I need that balance . . . I crave it . . . I am petrified of the raft going over the rapids. And that is why I simply can't invite your friends in."

I walked back to Tony and Evie. I explained

the situation. It was decided they would wait for me in the lobby.

As it turned out, it was very lucky that Weathers had not allowed Tony to watch, for he would have collapsed with laughter as Carlos Weathers put on one of his most ludicrous shows.

Luckily, I was not the focus of Carlos Weathers's lunacy that morning. It was poor Gordon Seaver.

"You're *acting*, Gordon," he said in a very low, accusatory voice.

"Yes? And?"

"You're *acting*. That's not what we want."

"And what do we want?"

"We want the truth. We don't want lines."

Gordon stared at me as if trying to enlist my sympathy. He had it. I couldn't speak for Gordon, but I hadn't heard such bald-faced pseudo-Stanislavski tripe in twenty years.

"But since the whole performance is going to be merely a working rehearsal—what the hell does it matter what I say? The performance is going to be about the interaction between director—you—and the actor—me. Right, Carlos?"

"Half right, Gordon. Because every moment of this experiment has to be authentic."

"You mean authentic Gordon or authentic Tennessee Williams?"

"Either way. Six of one . . ."

"All right. I'm yours," Gordon said sarcastically. "Authentic me."

"First of all, I don't like the way you're standing. Stand like a young man. Like the young stud Chance."

"But I'm old," Gordon said.

"Precisely. Let the conflict sink into the audience. Let them be shocked by an older man trying to play a younger man. Let the pathos depress them."

"Sure, Carlos. Anything you say."

"Remember, the secret is to grope."

"What?"

"Grope. To look at the lines as if they are totally confusing . . . as if you have to interpret them . . . as if you can't remember them. Groping is authenticity."

"Exactly," I said—with a straight face.

"Good. You know what I mean, Alice, don't you? Right? Good! Now, let's get on with it!"

But he couldn't get on with it, because Gordon's inability to "grope" seemed to obsess him and he kept going back to that concept. The concept of groping . . . of groping for lines and for the truth. Then he gave Gordon a lecture about Brando. About what had made Brando such a great actor in his youth . . . because he would grope. He would use the prompter even though he knew the lines cold. He would squint his eyes as if trying to make out the strange language.

I folded my arms and waited. The rehearsal was totally unreal to me. Not only because it was nonsense . . . but because I was no longer in Atlantic City as an actress . . . I was there as an investigator. Two people had been murdered. My task now was not dramaturgical; it was simply to find out who had committed the murders. And there was another reason for the unreality, for the sheer extent of the unreality.

And that reason was Harlow. That old black magic was beginning to get me in its spell.

Harlow was no joke. Stroke her and you won money. Stroke her a lot and you won a lot of money. But what was the downside of all this? What if there was something else accompanying all that luck? What if the other shoe hadn't dropped yet?

I knew that Tony felt we were in deep water also. Imagine inviting him to spend the night with me and not having to fight him off. The gambling had totally suspended Tony's libido. We seemed to be in a state of inquisitive quietude, as if no matter what happened, there had to be some explanation for his gambling success other than the mere stroking of a feline, eleven times. There had to be. No, Tony was not having an easy time with it.

Only Evie remained unfazed by it all. The cat's magic seemed, oddly enough, perfectly rational to her.

And apparently she had no trouble believing that two people were slaughtered for it.

I turned my attention to the "gropers."

After that dreadful rehearsal, I collected Tony and Evie in the lobby and we walked to Castles via the boardwalk. It was cold and windy, yes, but the sun was brilliant . . . flinging out bursts of warmth. One felt invigorated. One felt strong.

We found Lyle Sweetnum in a lounge, feet up, reading the newspaper.

He glared at us as we surrounded him and pulled up chairs at his table. Still not speaking, he folded his paper and lit a cigarette.

"I want to ask you some more questions about our mutual friend," I said.

"Who is that?"

"You know, Cleopatra."

He didn't respond. He was becoming nervous . . . I could see that. He kept trying to evaluate Tony . . . who was silent . . . and perhaps a bit threatening.

"I told you everything I know about her."

"But you didn't tell me her real name."

"I didn't know her name."

"That's hard to believe."

"Believe what you want."

"You told me you were friendly with her. You told me she was a lovely woman. You told me you had borrowed money from her."

"Yes."

"Then it's not plausible that you didn't know her name. At least her first name."

"This is Atlantic City. People have conversations with each other for hours . . . weeks . . . and there are no names used. I knew who she was. She knew who I was."

"Another thing bothers me, Lyle."

"What's that?"

"You told me you had heard of the murder."

"I had."

"From whom?"

"I don't remember."

"You see, Lyle, it wasn't in the papers. And besides, she wasn't wearing her wig in the Monte Carlo. How would anyone recognize her as the Cleopatra woman? Even you had to be helped a little picking her out from that photo I showed you—where she didn't have the wig on."

"Someone told me she was murdered."

"And you don't remember who at all?"

"No. Who the hell are you, anyway? A cop?"

"I told you before, I was a friend."

"Listen. In Atlantic City, everybody knows everything. Someone drops dead in one casino, twenty seconds later a washroom attendant on the other side of the boardwalk seems to know about it. And know what the guy did for a living, how much he had lost, and his extracurricular activities. That's just the way it is."

I sat back and stared at the young dealer. I didn't really know what to think of him. I searched Evie's face for a clue . . . to see how she was responding . . . but she was impassive. In spite of Sweetnum's lack of cooperation with us, Evie didn't seem to look upon him as a villain. I tended to trust her instincts.

Ordinarily I'd have been interested in Tony's instincts as well. But not now. Tony's thoughts were obviously not on Lyle Sweetnum and solving the two murders. He was staring out at the gambling pit. He looked like a starving dog being tormented by the aroma of roasting meat. It dawned on me that I might have created a monster in bringing Basillio down here.

"I remember, Lyle, that you told me you warned Cleopatra."

"Yes, I warned her. Damn right I warned her."

"After she had given you money."

"She didn't give me money. She lent it to me."

"Did you ever pay her back?"

"I didn't get the chance."

"Refresh my memory. Why did you warn her?"

"Because of that cat. Because people were going to want that cat. She was always bragging about it . . . about its power."

"Did you actually believe someone would kill her for the cat?"

"Yes, I did. But that wasn't the only reason I warned her. She was under a lot of pressure."

"What kind of pressure?"

"From the casinos."

"Because of the cat?"

"No. Because she was winning."

"I don't understand."

"What is there to understand? The casinos don't like people who win all the time. Not only don't they like it; they don't believe anyone *can* win all the time—not honestly."

"So they thought Cleopatra was cheating."

"Right. That she had some kind of scam going. Either some kind of new system or a connection with a crooked dealer."

"A crooked dealer," I repeated. "Yes, I can see how aligning yourself with a crooked dealer would work."

"I don't like what you're implying, lady. I was not in any kind of scam with Cleopatra. It wasn't like that."

"All right, Lyle. Let's continue. Tell me, what could the casinos do about it if they thought she was doing something crooked?"

"Ban her."

"Is that legal?"

"The casinos own Atlantic City. What they do is legal."

"Was she ever banned?"

"Well, yes, she was. But then something happened to change their minds—I don't know what—and she was allowed to play again. But they watched her like a hawk."

"Her real name was Adele Houghton." I don't know why I told the dealer that, but I watched his face anxiously, as if something would happen. It didn't.

All he said in response was, "She was a very good person."

"Did she play roulette?" Tony asked.

"Not often."

"Did she win when she did play?"

"She won at everything. Roulette. Baccarat. You name it."

"Craps, too?"

"Yes."

Tony shook his head in wonderment. I could see that he was itching to be at the tables again.

"But," Lyle added, "her specialty really was blackjack."

Basillio laughed out loud. "Isn't that a coincidence?"

"I have to go to work," Lyle said abruptly. He snuffed out the cigarette violently. He stood then, and walked off without another word.

"What happens next?" Tony asked.

"We find the apartment she kept in Atlantic City."

"Look in the phone book."

"Under what, Tony?"

"Under Houghton, comma, Adele."

"Don't be a pinhead, Tony. Don't you think I've looked? There is no Adele Houghton in the Atlantic City phone book."

"Then you'll never find it."

"We'll find it if we put our thinking caps on," I retorted.

Apparently, Evie appreciated my old-fashioned phrase. "That's the spirit," she said, patting me gently on the arm. "Be positive. You can make it if you try, like the old song says. Just put that thinking cap on and you'll find a way."

"Just what's in her apartment that you want to find it so badly?" Tony asked.

"I have no idea."

"Then what's the point?"

"The point is one remaining thread. Break it and Carmella will be convicted of murder. Listen to me, Tony: Carmella didn't kill her friend Adele. And no bookmaker killed Art Agee. If we don't keep hold of the string, if we don't keep following it, then nothing will come out right. No justice, Tony. No beauty. No truth."

"Okay. Take it easy, Swede. You don't have to give me that truth, beauty, and justice spiel. I know what I have to do."

"So let's get to work. All of us. Right here. First of all, what do we know for sure?"

"Well," Tony said, "we know she lived two lives in two places. As a labor lawyer in Manhattan. As a gambler in Atlantic City."

"Right."

"And that's all we know."

"Well, I think we can figure out where she lived in Atlantic City. I mean, in a general sense."

"Like where?"

"Close to the casinos. Close to the gambling. If she was handling a double life, she had to be close to the action on this end."

"That is for sure," said Evie.

"That doesn't narrow it too much," Tony said. "There are a bunch of little streets that run into the boardwalk. They're full of small two-family houses. It's a nowhere place to live—just the casinos on one side and the main shopping street on the other."

"Yes. So, say she lived in one of those houses on one of those streets. The streets run between the boardwalk and the main street. And it is a nowhere place to live, as you say. All of that gives us good reason to assume neighborhood people get everything they need on that main street. Therefore, that's where Adele shopped."

"Why don't we just pick up the damn voodoo cat and wander around? Maybe she'll find her own place for us. If she can win all that money for us, she sure as hell can find where she was living."

"An interesting theory, Tony, but impractical."

"That never stopped you before."

"There's another thing we can count on. That she used the name Adele."

"How do you know that?"

"It just makes sense. Let's say I was in her shoes. I definitely wouldn't use my real last name, but I would use my first name, my real one, with the bogus last name."

"Why?"

"Because, first of all, if one slipped up it didn't matter. She always got half of her phony name right. Besides, she could still use the phony name with her credit card if she ran into financial difficulty. All she had to do was claim that the phony name was her maiden name and her card was under her married name."

"It does make sense," Evie agreed.

"So," I added up what we had, "Adele lived on one of the blocks near the casino and she continued to use her real first name."

It wasn't much. We all sat there and brooded.

"She must have come down from Manhattan every weekend and a couple of nights a week," Tony suggested.

"Probably," I agreed.

"Where did she keep Harlow?" Evie asked.

Her question scrambled some wires in my head. "Listen!" I said excitedly. "Her friends claim Adele had no cat. If her friends aren't lying, that means she kept Harlow all the time in Atlantic City. She never brought Harlow into Manhattan."

"How could she do that?" Tony asked.

"She couldn't do it. Unless . . ." I grinned a big fat cheshire cat grin ". . . unless she had someone like me."

Evie was confused. "Someone like you? What does that mean?"

"I am a cat-sitter in my spare time," I explained.

Tony jumped in. "You mean she kept the cat in her Atlantic City apartment all the time. And when she wasn't here she used a sitter for that million-dollar bundle of voodoo bones."

"Exactly."

Tony deflated. "I don't see how that helps us."

"Well, we think she lived and shopped near the casino. So there has to be a pet supply store on the main street. It's plain that Adele took very good care of that cat. Probably bought vitamins and special food additives and cat toys and so on. Maybe she fed her a special brand of cat food . . . something the supermarkets don't carry. So, if you're a regular at a pet store, you probably know about people who sit with animals. Isn't that logical? Isn't it?"

"What do we do?"

"What do *you* do, Tony? You take a walk into the shopping area . . . it's only two blocks west of the boardwalk. You find a pet store. You buy a cat carrier. And while you are purchasing the carrier you engage the salesperson in conversation."

"About what?"

"Think, young man, think," Evie lectured. "You want to locate the best cat-sitter around."

"Exactly. Thank you, Evie," said I.

"And you want me to go now?"

"Yes, Tony. Immediately."

He looked over hungrily at the casino pit. He looked like a sad trapped beast. "There are millions of dollars slipping through our fingers, Swede, at this very moment."

"Get to the pet store, Tony, or you'll never stroke another of my cats."

He saluted and backed out of the door.

"You ought to keep an eye on him," Evie cautioned. "He doesn't keep his mind on his business."

Chapter 14

Evie and I went into the casino pit to play video poker a bit while Tony was on his errand. But we hadn't stroked Harlow. And we lost. Both of us.

"Do you think there is a time limit on the potency of her magic?" I asked Evie. "Do you think the magic wears off after eleven hours and then you have to stroke her again?"

The minute I asked those questions I felt like a fool. I was beginning to believe too wholeheartedly. This madness had a limit. I realized I better get my rational hemisphere into gear or I really was going to end up sticking pins in dolls.

Evie said in reply: "Nothing is forever."

"Did Cleopatra ever gamble in the morning, like we're doing?"

"I think she was a night lady," Evie replied.

Yes, I thought, that's the way it probably was with Adele. It was a fantasy in her very structured life. And suddenly the crevice began to open . . . and she started slipping down. And there was money. Legally. More money than she had ever seen in her life. She was probably very generous. She had made a loan to Lyle. Maybe she gave away thousands . . . hundreds of thousands . . . millions . . . maybe she gave money to Art Agee. He owed bookmakers, the police said. Maybe she gave money to bums, derelicts, political causes. But she always kept the line between gambler and lawyer. No one knew. Or did they? I had to get into her apartment.

Evie started winning. I kept losing. I stopped playing. I looked around. It was only about ten o'clock in the morning but the machines were well patronized. This was a world I could not fathom.

"Were you ever married, Evie?" I asked, trying to get back to the real world.

"Three times," she said. "Two died and one vanished."

"Were they gamblers?"

"I wouldn't marry a sporting man," she said.

"But, Evie, you gamble ferociously."

"Women can handle it. Men can't. If I had loved one of them, maybe I would have let him. But they were marriages of convenience. Mine. They thought the other way around. Both hoaxing each other. Not the way to live, young woman."

Sometimes Evie's wisdom was so complex I was struck dumb.

I went back into the lounge and left Evie at the video poker game. But I watched her from where I sat. What an elegant old lady she was. I wondered if I would survive to that age and, if I did, whether I would have the ability to manipulate any machine . . . much less a gambling contraption like that one.

She saw me looking and waved. I waved back.

She fixed her hat. She was always doing that. She carried long gloves in her purse but she never put them on.

I closed my eyes and tried to nap. A quick morning nap was always a good idea. But it didn't work. The buzz in the casino was too persistent. When I opened my eyes Evie had returned and was seated near me.

"He is taking his time," said Evie.

"Maybe he got lost. He doesn't do well in strange towns."

"You can't get lost in Atlantic City," said Evie. "It's laid out like a Monopoly board."

That's right. I had forgotten all about that. Atlantic and Pacific avenues. It was the inspiration for the game of Monopoly.

At last, an unhappy Tony appeared. He was carrying an enormous package.

He dropped the wrapped bundle down in front of me.

"I found a pet shop. But the selection was lousy. I mean, we need a very posh carrier for Madame Voodoo, don't we? This was the best I could get."

He squatted down and ripped the paper off. It was a lovely carrier . . . almost all leather . . . with mesh sides and top, so that the cat could see everything.

"What about the cat-sitter, Tony?" I asked, pushing the carrier away from me a bit with my foot.

"Well, my source tells me that there is only one authentic, read responsible, cat-sitter in downtown Atlantic City . . . which is, according to her, where we are . . . and that is the assistant manager of the Laundromat, whose name is Billy."

"Billy who?"

"I don't know."

"Where is the Laundromat?"

"Two stores next to the pet store."

"And Billy's in there now?"

"So the lady in the pet store said."

"Sit down for a minute, Tony." He sat. I started to explain what I had in mind.

"First I want to go back to my room and get some kind of appropriate clothes on."

"Appropriate to what?" Tony asked.

"As if I were a friend of Adele, a lawyer, from New York."

"I don't get it."

"You see, Adele asked me to do her a favor: to bring her cat back to Atlantic City . . . to her apartment. There had been a veterinary checkup in Manhattan, which is why the cat was there. Well, on the train I lost the damn envelope that carried the keys and the apartment address. So here I am in Atlantic City with Adele's cat and I can't get to her apartment because I don't have either the address or the key . . . and I can't contact Adele because she is somewhere in California on business. But I do remember that she always talked about this wonderful cat-sitter named Billy. . . ."

"Brilliant, Swede. Goddamn brilliant, if you can pull it off."

Evie didn't respond, but she kept nodding appreciatively.

"I'll go into the Laundromat alone, with Harlow in the carrier," I said, "but I'd like both of you to be in a rented car following me."

"We'll need another car . . . the police have the last one."

"Yes. I understand that. Let Tony rent it this time."

"My credit card is up to the limit."

"Put it on the card and then pay in cash. You still have all that money, don't you, Tony?"

"Uh . . . Of course."

"Tony, if you've been gambling with—"

"No, no, no. Really. I've got it covered."

"If everything goes well," I said, "we'll be in Cleopatra's apartment within the hour."

"Yes . . . *if* she used the name Adele in Atlantic City like you believe . . . and *if* Harlow is really her cat and *if* Billy was her sitter. Otherwise you'll be nowhere."

Let's face it. Once in a while Tony makes a good point. Even Evie's face registered that.

"There it is! There it is!" An anxious Tony leaned over from the backseat, pointing.

Evie pulled the rented car up to the curb, between the pet store and the Laundromat. Harlow was resting on my lap, in her new carrier. She seemed totally unconcerned . . . almost reflective.

"Wait and watch," I said.

Tony laughed. "You sound like some kind of religious nut, Swede. Wait and watch for what?"

I climbed out of the car and walked into the Laundromat, dressed in my conception of lady lawyer travel outfit, holding the leather carrier firmly in my right hand.

I projected calm but that wasn't the way I was feeling. I was suspended on a kind of anticipation . . . as if I were looking down on the whole mess from a slow-moving plane.

The Laundromat was not crowded. It was a long and narrow store with the machines lined up along the walls and all kinds of rolling receptacles in the aisles.

Two kinds of services were offered, or so I surmised from the sign over the cash register: JUST DO IT . . . OR LET US.

The prices were chalked up on a large board. I checked out the wash and fold price. Much less than in Manhattan.

Halfway down the long store, two people stood and chatted over a whirring machine. One of them was a tall young man . . . heavyset . . . wearing his baseball cap backward. Emblematic of something, but what?

"Are you Billy the cat-sitter?" I called out.

He nodded and then held up a hand, signifying that he would join me in a minute. I put the carrier on a nearby table and stood by it, waiting.

When he headed toward me I noticed he was wearing red sneakers with the laces untied.

"Look," I said, "this is a very embarrassing situation for me. And I need your help. If you are the Billy I'm looking for. Billy the cat-sitter?"

"I sure am Billy. And I sure am a cat-sitter, lady," he said in an even, friendly tone.

I began to tell him the prepared story. He seemed to be listening, but his interest was on the cat carrier and the beast within.

Just as I approached the ending of the

tragedy . . . how I had left the envelope with the keys and address of Adele's apartment on the train . . . he gave out a kind of war whoop.

Then he said excitedly: "It's Miss Otis!" And he repeated: "Miss Otis!" Then he opened the carrier and picked up Harlow, kissed her, and draped her around his neck. Harlow, aka Miss Otis, looked positively ecstatic. Obviously, I had come to the right place.

"Come on back here," he said, walking, draped, to the rear of the store. I followed him. He unlocked a small wooden wall closet. Inside were rows of hooks and on each hook was a set of keys and a tag identifying it.

He plucked one from the wall and gave it to me. "The address is on the tag. It's only two blocks away."

I took the key.

"But I can't leave the store, Miss. Why don't you just deliver Miss Otis yourself and bring the key back to me."

He walked me back to the front of the store and dumped Miss Otis lovingly back into her carrier. "I love to take care of her," he said.

Holding the key and accompanying tag like a war trophy I walked out of the Laundromat and toward Adele's apartment, watching the street signs and keeping sight of the car following me.

Five minutes later I was fumbling at a door on the side of a very small, ugly, two-story house, half stucco, half brick, that had obviously been built a long time ago and showed the effects of the wind and rain and brine from the nearby ocean.

It was hard to open. Tony and Evie stood in back of me. Tony held the carrier. I was so flushed with the success of my scheme vis-à-vis Billy the cat-sitter that I felt I could kick the door in if the key didn't work.

But there was no need for violence. The key clicked. The door opened, and we all walked inside.

Tony flicked on the wall light.

My triumph died away fast because Adele's apartment was so damn grim and small and ugly.

It was a one-room box with a bathroom and an alcove kitchen.

There were large windows but no light entered because the huge casinos, only half a block away, shut out everything.

"You would think that a million-dollar kitty could afford more," Tony said.

I opened the carrier and Harlow bounded out. She ran around a bit. She looked here and there. She pranced. She preened. It was obvious she was home and very happy about it.

The room was sparsely furnished. There

was a divan along one wall. A high ten-drawer chest against another wall. A beat-up coffee table and a sling chair. A small television set on the floor, plugged into a wall socket.

There were two scatter rugs on the floor.

One closet—right next to the door. Inside were mops and brooms and a vacuum cleaner, and several winter garments.

Evie sat down on the divan. Tony sat next to her. I sat down on the sling chair. We all watched Harlow as she happily prowled her home.

"Okay. We're here. It was brilliant, Swede. That whole thing with Billy the cat-sitter. So what? What do we do now?"

"Something's in this room, Tony," I said.

"What?"

"I don't know yet."

"Well, I hope this is not one of your romantic delusions, Swede."

"Like Harlow?" I countered him. He shut up.

Yes, I thought, staring around at the ugly box of a room, *it* is *here*.

If it wasn't here . . . then everything would fade away. If it wasn't here . . . nothing would be revealed . . . cleaned up . . . understood.

"You will agree this whole mess demands clarification?" I shouted at Tony. He nodded. Get hold of yourself, Alice, I cautioned myself silently. I looked at Evie. She was calm, comfortable. Harlow had joined her on the divan. Why not? This was her apartment.

"The closet first," I said.

I searched the pockets and seams of every garment in the closet. I searched the walls. I shook out the mops and brooms. Nothing.

"I am looking for something, Tony," I explained, "that ties Cleopatra to Adele Houghton. It has to be here. And that bloody object, whatever it is, will tie Cleopatra to the person who murdered her . . . and probably murdered Art Agee as well."

"Clear as a bell," said Tony. He shooed Evie and Harlow off the divan.

He started to run his hands carefully over the fabric.

Evie walked over to the large chest with ten drawers, opened the top one and let out a yell.

I rushed over.

"Look!" she ordered. I peered over her shoulder. There were about ten Cleopatra-type wigs.

"Adele had a wig problem," I said.

Then, together, Evie and I emptied the other nine drawers. Nothing. Nothing. Blank. Some clothes. Some towels. Some trinkets. Some sheets. Nothing identifiable or quirky or different or revealing. Nothing.

Time was moving. I had to bring the keys

back to Billy in the Laundromat. He would become suspicious if I stayed too long.

"Do the bathroom, Tony!"

He followed orders impeccably.

"Evie! Help me move this."

We pulled the chest away from the wall. I was so intent on my mission that I had completely forgotten Evie was probably almost eighty years old. We inspected each drawer. Nothing. My clock was beginning to race. I felt a depression approaching me like a tidal wave.

"Let's do the kitchen."

Evie opened the oven. One pan. One roll of aluminum foil. Nothing else. I looked under the small sink. Nothing. Evie opened the kitchen cabinets.

Nothing. Except for twelve cans of cat food. Two piles—six in each.

"Nothing in the bathroom," Tony declared.

"Were you careful?" I challenged.

"Like a vacuum cleaner," he said.

I remembered the vacuum cleaner in the closet. I went back and dismantled it. Nothing.

We were all getting a bit crazed. Where else could we look? No place.

"There doesn't seem to be anything here," Evie said.

"We did our best," Tony said.

I felt numb. I felt stupid. I had taken it so

far. I had put all my eggs into this basket because there simply was no other basket . . . no other eggs. A manic-depressive woman named Carmella, sits in a jail cell accused of the murder of Adele Houghton. A bookmaker somewhere in Philadelphia or New York, whom I never met or could even hope to meet, is probably about to be charged with the murder of Art Agee. What did they mean to me? Nothing. I played the cards I had and suddenly there was the perception it might not have been a winning hand. But I had no choice.

"It's time to go," Tony repeated solicitously. Then he added: "You can't win 'em all."

"Yes. There is nothing here," Evie intoned.

For some reason her tone infuriated me. I stared at her as if I were seeing her for the first time.

The thought came to me that I had trusted her far too much and far too easily . . . that I never should have suggested a vacation to her after I won all that money . . . that I never should have gotten her a room next to mine . . . that I really knew nothing about her . . . that she was a very strange old lady . . . that it was entirely possible she was part of a murder conspiracy.

Was there anyone I did trust in this mess now?

"Let me get Harlow," I said, "and then we'll go."

I scooped up Harlow and put her back into the carrier. She was none too happy about it and I didn't blame her. Poor thing. On the road again.

Then I headed toward the door where Evie and Tony were waiting.

"Shouldn't we fix the place up?" Tony asked, pointing to the disruptions of our search.

"Why? She's dead." My response was bitter.

Just as I was about to close the door behind me, I recalled the cans of cat food. It would be stupid to leave them.

"I'll be right back," I told the others.

I rushed into the kitchen, grabbed all twelve cans, and headed for the door.

I stopped.

Something was odd.

I dropped the cans on the coffee table. It made a dreadful noise.

Evie and Tony came rushing back inside. "What's going on?" he asked.

I didn't answer. I was separating the cans. Six of them were simply unopened cans of cat food.

The other six were far too light; closed with plastic lids . . . the kind that manufacturers often supply to keep the food fresh after the can has been opened.

It was as if someone had opened the cans, emptied the contents, and then closed the lid.

"These seem to be empty," I said, holding one in my hand. It was light as air.

"Why saves empty cans?" Evie wondered aloud.

Tony grabbed it out of my hand. "But it isn't empty," he said, rattling it a little.

He held the can up to the light. Then he pulled the plastic lid off.

Tony shook the can out over the coffee table.

Out fell a carefully folded, delicate white handkerchief.

I spread the handkerchief open.

Inside was a small snapshot going brown around the edges.

Each of the other five "empty" cans held a similar package.

There were six photos in all, all obviously taken around the same time and place—at the beach—perhaps even on the same day. The same two young men appeared in every photograph. In one, they are standing. In another, they're sitting next to each other on the sand. In one they are about to go into the water. In another, they are joined by two young women in post-World War II casual clothing.

"Let's get back to the hotel—fast," I said, gathering up the treasure trove.

* * *

Feeling guilty about all the involuntary exercise I'd put her through, I packed Evie off to her room for a rest.

Harlow was sulking because I had disturbed her nap on my bed and resettled her in the chair.

I was displaying our find on the taut quilt.

Tony and I stared down at the objects.

Six handkerchiefs. And six old photographs.

"Monograms," said Tony. "Hey, this is the kind of handkerchief mothers used to give their sons when they stepped out into the world. Back in my day, anyway."

"Can you read the monograms?"

"It looks like . . . A.A. Something tells me those letters don't stand for Alcoholics Anonymous."

"Art Agee," I pronounced solemnly.

I studied the two men in the photos. Each seemed to be about twenty years old.

One of them was stockier and darker complexioned than the other.

I kept looking at that one—the stocky one.

I had this funny feeling that I knew him . . . or I had met him . . . somewhere.

Tony picked up on that. "You know him?"

"I think so."

"From where?"

"I don't know. I keep getting closer and then it slips away. You know what I mean?"

"Someone from Minnesota? When you were a kid?"

"No. Not that."

"From New York."

"I don't know."

"Acting class! Was he in one of your classes?"

"No. Definitely not."

"A play somewhere? Off-Broadway."

"No."

"Cat-sitting then. Maybe he was a client."

"No. I'd remember that."

Tony was doing his best to help me. He kept firing the questions at me.

"From your movie fiasco in France?"

"Certainly not."

"Think, Swede. You were a little girl when that photograph was taken. Did you know him a long time ago? Maybe he was a family friend."

"No, no, Tony. Recently."

"He'd probably be about seventy by now, Swede."

"I don't care. I know that face. I've seen that face somewhere."

"Maybe here."

"What do you mean, '*here*'?"

"Exactly what I said. Here. In Atlantic City."

That stopped me cold.

"Tony! That's it!"

167

"Who is he?"

"The owner."

"What owner?"

"The owner of this casino—the Monte Carlo. His name, if I remember correctly, is Tobin Haggar."

"And what about the other guy? Do you know him, too?"

"I don't think so. He's not familiar at all."

"So you met this Haggar?"

"Yes. When Gordon Seaver and I first arrived. But only for a minute."

Tony glared at Harlow, who was conspiring to get back on the bed.

"Okay. So the person in the photo grew up to become the owner of this casino. What does it mean?"

"That I don't know."

"What are you going to do?"

"I think what we have to do is find out who the other man is."

"Great. How are we going to do that?"

It was a good question. I picked up one of the photographs and ripped it in half.

"Hey! What are you doing?"

I held the half containing the unidentified young man. Tobin Haggar had been extirpated.

Then I picked up the phone and asked the operator to get me the head of casino security, Charlie Lott. He wasn't in. Did I wish to leave a message? I said I wanted Mr. Lott to contact Detective Baretta of the Atlantic City Police; to tell him that I had some information for him and wanted to see him as soon as possible.

I hung up the phone, waited ten seconds, and picked it up again.

I asked for room service and ordered sandwich makings, fruit, wine, cookies, and coffee.

Then I gathered the nonmutilated photos and put them away, out of sight. I destroyed the ragged half photo of young Tobin Haggar and put the half containing the mystery man into my jacket pocket.

"That name isn't for real, is it?" Tony asked.

"Baretta? Yes. And don't you dare make any jokes when he gets here."

"So now what?"

"We wait for the food and we wait for Baretta."

"Are you going to show him only half a photograph?"

"Yes. That's all he deserves."

An hour and fifty minutes after I had left that message with the head of casino security, Detective Baretta knocked on my door.

He removed his hat as he entered, an oddly charming and old world custom. "No bodies?" he asked bemusedly.

"None at the moment, Detective Baretta."

"Charlie Lott told me you had something for me."

As I introduced him to Tony, Baretta stared at the remains of the room service feast.

"Help yourself," I offered.

He circled the cart and selected one sliver of pickle—which he chomped on, chewed, and swallowed.

Then, starting with one slice of rye bread, he built a mighty tower of salami and provolone. After that, he poured wine for himself.

"I don't ever want to hear another word about starving actors," he said.

Baretta wandered about the suite making silent fun of its overblown Atlantic City opulence.

Then he got down to business. "So what do you have for me?"

"A photograph," I said.

He shrugged.

"Here, take a peek," I said, and pushed the half of a photograph into his hand.

There was plenty of light in the early afternoon suite but for some reason Detective Baretta took the half of a photograph to the window.

Tony made himself another half a sandwich.

Baretta held the photo up and said with a chuckle: "Cute."

It was the last kind of comment I was expecting him to make. Cute?

He walked over and gave me the photo back.

"So?" he asked.

"Well, do you know who that is?"

"Of course. It's Ben Rios. Looks like it was taken on the beach here in Atlantic City— what? forty? fifty? some years ago. You can see the old steel pier in the distance."

Baretta grinned and added: "Why don't you send it to him? He's doing about two hundred years in the Trenton State Penitentiary. He'd appreciate it probably."

Tony materialized behind my shoulder.

"I don't know who Ben Rios is," I said, looking at the face. I was trying to match the young face . . . with someone . . . with anyone. Was this Ben Rios the father of the late Adele Houghton? Had Adele's double life and her involvement with the casino been part of some vendetta against Tobin Haggar? Or was there in that untroubled young face some resemblance to the murder suspect, Carmella Koteit? I suppose the young man in the photograph might just as well have become the father of Art Agee, or Lyle Sweetnum, or either of the two remaining members of the quartet of friends—the four lady blues musketeers who had come together every year for so many years, but would never be together again. I tried to bring Bliss Revere's face into focus. But all I could see in my mind's eye were those unfriendly black sunglasses. And when I thought of Joan Secunda, I saw only the anger in her eyes as she berated me for libeling poor dead Adele, and accused me of a little breaking and entering on the side.

Tony said, "He's a gangster. A wise guy. A bad man. From Newark." He turned to Baretta. "Right?"

"Exactly," the detective confirmed.

"Don't you remember him, Swede? About five years ago he was arrested for milking Broadway shows."

"No."

"That wasn't what he was sent up for," Baretta noted.

"How did he milk them, Tony?"

"Well, it was beautiful. Say a bunch of angels put up a couple of million for a show. Rios, through a producer, hired all kinds of theatrical consultants for the show, even before it opened. Like costume consultants, lighting consultants. They got ridiculous fees—$150,000 for eight minutes' work or something like that. The consultant then kicked it back to the producer who was working for Rios."

He started to wax poetic about the elegance of the scam.

I sshhh-ed him, holding my hand up to my lips.

Then I sat down very slowly, almost fastidiously, on the enormous bed. Tony and Baretta continued to talk, but I swept them into a corner of my mind while I pondered.

Was young Art Agee a sort of Broadway mobster? After all, it was he who came up with the idea for the Valentine's Day love program. That might have been nothing more than an elaborate cover for some other activity. But of course, something had gone terribly wrong, and Art had ended up dead.

Tony started to pace in front of me, gesturing as he spoke to Detective Baretta. I watched the nervous, back and forth movement of his feet. The movement reminded me of something else . . . of a distant conversation about walking up . . . no, not about walking, about taking the elevators . . . some debate about the safety of elevators and how one didn't have to worry in the Monte Carlo because if the elevators broke down there was free and easy access between floors. Art Agee had boasted of that to Gordon Seaver.

Now the floodgates of memory were opening. I remembered a whole lot of other conversations and movement. I remembered a middle-age man moving like a dancer. I re-

membered a murder suspect humming a
tune. I remembered a successful diet clinic
entrepreneur who seemed able to change ap-
pearances like a 19th-century actress. And I
remembered the wigs in Adele's apartment.
As if each one represented a spectacular gambling coup. With the help of Miss Otis.

I got up and opened the window. I looked
up and then down, as I had that night when
Harlow hopped into my life, trying to figure
out where she'd come from. I looked out and
saw the pounding winter surf. I could almost
hear the ocean singing.

My fingers were starting to tingle. Really
tingle. Was the answer in the waves? No,
nothing so otherworldly. The answer—or an-
swers—were coming from within. They
sprang from my own garbled memories. It
came to me that I might be able to end this
whole mess now, because of a song. *Because
it might be all about that bloody tune.*

I turned around and stared at the two men.
Yes . . . it had all boiled down to one lousy
song. I knew that I could end it now. Not in
days . . . but in hours.

"I am starting to worry about you, Swede.
You're acting a little peculiar."

"Winners like us, Tony . . . big win-
ners . . . can act any damn way they want.
That's what gambling is all about. Freedom.
Isn't that correct, Detective Baretta?"

"I don't gamble," the detective said.

"I'm sure you have other vices to compensate," I replied.

"You are correct."

"But you do know Atlantic City, don't you?"

"Which Atlantic City are you talking about?" Baretta asked a bit sarcastically. "There are two cities here. The city of casinos and the city of everyone else. The first city is rich. The second is dirt poor."

"The casinos."

"Yes, I know the casinos."

"Is it true about the interconnectedness?"

"What language is that?"

"I mean, is it true that if someone sneezes at a dice table in a casino at one end of the boardwalk, someone says 'God bless you' at a table at the other end of the boardwalk?"

"I suppose it is. News travels fast in that world."

I was beginning to feel a palpable excitement.

"Tell me, Detective Baretta, are you coming off your shift or going on it?"

"Off."

"If I made it worthwhile to you, would you work a few hours overtime? Right here?"

Detective Baretta threw a look full of puzzlement, and some panic, Tony's way.

"Worthwhile how?" he finally asked. "What are you talking about?"

I walked around the food table. I had a sense of absolute clairvoyant power . . . that I could orchestrate everything that would happen . . . that I knew precisely what I was doing.

Baretta took another sliver of pickle. Tony took a small slice of meat, put some coleslaw on it, then rolled it like sushi and ate.

"I can give you the killer," I said.

He almost choked on his pickle. He wiped his hands with a cloth napkin carefully.

"What killer are you talking about?"

"The one who killed Adele Houghton and Art Agee."

"I think you're confused. The woman who killed Adele Houghton is currently in jail. The murderers of Art Agee haven't been charged yet—and they don't have anything to do with the first murder."

"No. *You're* confused, Detective."

"Show me how."

"That's what I want to do. Within the next couple of hours someone is going to break into the room next door."

"Why?"

"Because there is something very valuable in there. And the person who'll break in is the same person who slashed Adele Houghton to death and shot Art Agee."

"Let me get this straight. You want me to

stay here and just wait for this big event to happen?"

"Yes."

Detective Baretta shook his head and laughed. He started to pursue the food again, confused as to how to respond.

But meanwhile Tony was pulling at my arm and whispering in my ear: "What the hell are you up to, Swede? There's a million-dollar kitty in the room next door. You don't want to lose her. She's also a damn pretty kitty."

"It's not the cat they're after," I said.

"Are you kidding?"

"Listen to me, Tony. We don't have time for this kind of conversation now. I need your help."

He stepped back and nodded.

"Get a pencil and a piece of paper, sit down, and write out all the lyrics to 'Every Honey Has Her Harry.'"

He stared at me, not saying a word.

"Did you hear me, Tony?" I was speaking low so that Detective Baretta would have difficulty hearing.

"Please, Basillio!" I said urgently, cutting him off before he could ask the inevitable *have you lost your mind?* "Just do what I ask. Write down all the lyrics you remember."

"How about 'Blue Swede Shoes,' too?"

I turned my attention back to a perplexed Baretta. "The way I see it, Detective, you have absolutely nothing to lose. If I'm right, the murderer will fall into your lap. And it's pleasant enough here, isn't it?"

He looked at me for a long time and then, still not responding, sauntered over to where Tony was seated, writing furiously on a sheet of the hotel's ornate stationery. I waited while they exchanged a few whispered words—with my sanity, no doubt, the topic of conversation.

That detective was beginning to irritate me . . . to frustrate me . . . but I kept cool. I had bigger fish to fry and he was just a net.

"All done, you two?" I asked calmly.

"Yes, ma'am," Baretta said. "I've got to be honest. I just had to ask homeboy over there if you were crazy."

"That's right, Detective. Always go to the source." I glanced over at Basillio, who was very hard at work with his scribblings.

"He said the cops in New York call you the Cat Woman."

"Thank you for that, Tony." Basillio refused to meet my eyes.

"He said," the detective went on, "you've basically got all your marbles, but you often indulge in these kinds of schemes. Apparently your feline nature gives you the irresistible urge to set traps . . . to stalk."

"Anything else?"

"Said you often seem not to know what

you're doing. But sometimes the traps work anyway. Maybe fifty percent of the time, he said."

Time was wasting and I still had to speak with Evie, alone. The trap could not be set without her help.

Then Tony looked up at Baretta and called out to him: "You're in for a dime. Might as well be in for a dollar."

Baretta thought about it a minute, then nodded his head in assent.

Male bonding at work. It did have its uses.

"You're on," Detective Baretta said. "But please . . . no more food. I can't control my-self around pickles."

I walked over to Tony.

"I have maybe half of it," he said, looking up from his labors.

"Keep at it. And I need some of that money you won."

"How much?"

"Twenty-five hundred-dollar bills with a rubber band around them."

Tony grabbed my hand and kissed it, making a little purring sound at the same time. "Like they say on Broadway, madam: 'What-ever Lola wants' . . ."

Chapter 15

It was only forty-five minutes later that Evie Soames and I sat at a small table close to the bandstand of the bar in Surf World.

In my purse was the twenty-five hundred dollars. Also in my purse was an index card on which was printed:

"It is a great honor to call up on stage Miss Evie Soames. She is staying at the Monte Carlo up the boardwalk, but she's smart enough to party at Surf World. If the name doesn't ring a bell . . . don't be embarrassed. But insiders know all about her . . . because she was the real life hootchy-kootchy girl on whom the lead role in that legendary Broadway musical, *Pie in Your Face*, was based. And she sang 'Every Honey Has Her Harry' in gin joints a long time ago. Let's give her a big hand."

And in Evie's pocket was Basillio's recollection of the lyrics for "Every Honey." It didn't really matter how true to the original song it was—as long as it had some resemblance.

Underneath the lines, Tony had written: "Sung to the music of 'Diamonds Are a Girl's Best Friend,' leavened by a dose of bump and grind music." Since there was no sheet music available and it had long vanished from popular melody memory, Tony's squib was invaluable.

"What would you like?" I asked Evie.

"Something very strong."

"How about tequila and orange juice?"

"A Tequila Sunrise. That sounds good."

I ordered it, and a club soda for myself. We stared at the bandstand. This time the young singer was a tall young woman in a frilly dress who was singing a lot of pop, a lot of country, and some country rock. She was backed up by two guitarists, a drummer, and a keyboard.

The drinks came.

"Are you nervous?" I asked.

"A bit."

"If you can't do it, Evie, I'll understand."

"I agreed to do it and I will do it. Besides, I'm not *really* nervous. I'm way too old to be scared anymore, Alice. I think I just don't want to look too stupid. Besides, I can't really sing."

"It doesn't matter what you sound like. Believe me. You'll dazzle them just by standing up there."

The drinks came. We toasted our success.

"You sure do think up some wild enjoyments," Evie said. I didn't respond but I truly hoped that Evie didn't really believe I had orchestrated this entire thing for enjoyment . . . for fun . . . for kicks.

The singer went into what was actually a very interesting version of "Your Cheating Heart"—part punk rock and part Saturday night in Appalachia.

There were only about ten customers in the bar area, most of them at tables. On the side of the bandstand was a sign announcing this group as Mae Jolly and the Band-Aids.

I was getting nervous. Very nervous. This was, as they say, crunch time.

Mae Jolly finished the song, sang one more, and then announced she was going to take a little break. The singer and the musicians trudged off the stage and filed past our table.

I motioned wildly to the singer. She seemed to be sleepwalking. One of the band members poked her. She came over, smiling one of those "here we go again" smiles. She said "howdy," as if she were a real cowgirl, but the accent was definitely California.

"Could you just join us for one minute . . ." I implored.

She slid into the seat. She looked very tired and very unhappy.

"Mae, right?"

"Mae Jolly," she affirmed.

"I'm Alice Nestleton and this is Evie Soames," I said and I could see Mae cringe with a kind of "what's coming next?"

I had planned to present the plan in stages. But this singer looked so disgruntled that I decided to cut loose without any preliminaries whatsoever.

I pulled the announcement card out of my purse and slid it in front of the singer. Then I pulled out the wad of hundreds and ripped off the rubber band.

"Could you read that? It'll only take a moment," I said.

Mae read it. Then she stared at Evie.

Mae sat back, exasperated. "Look . . . both of you . . . I don't know the song and I don't know that Broadway play, but I'm sure you're a wonderful singer and everybody here would be happy to see you and hear you."

She shoved the card back. "But I can't invite anybody up on the stage. They won't go for that. They'd fire me."

"No, they won't," I said. "They don't care what you do onstage."

She folded her arms and shook her head.

I took the wad of bills and very carefully,

right in front of her, in a quiet voice, counted out the twenty-five hundreds.

"If you take that card, Mae, and go up on the stage after your break, and read the card, and Evie goes up and sings a few bars—it's all yours."

I rewrapped the bills and put the wad into her palm.

"Are you serious? You're giving me all this money to do one intro from the audience. And she only wants to sing a couple of bars?"

"Yes."

She kept shaking her head from side to side, staring at Evie and then at me. Finally, she read my card over again, grinned, and said: "Let's hootchy-kootchy."

We drove slowly along the street just west of Casino Row. Evie, at the wheel, was as happy as any supper club diva at the end of a first-night triumph.

"Well?" she said. "So what did you think, Alice? How was I?"

"You knocked them out, Evie."

"You know, it felt really good up there. And my voice wasn't bad. I mean, I didn't have any time to prepare. . . ."

"Take a right here, Evie."

"Why? Don't you want to go back to the Monte Carlo? I thought we're going to catch a murderer."

"We are. But now that we've added the yeast, the bread has to rise. Let's ride around a bit."

We drove away from the boardwalk.

"How long will it take the bread to rise?"

"I figure an hour. I figure within the hour everyone in Atlantic City who is interested will know that you performed that song from that musical on stage at Surf World."

"But who will care?"

"Someone who'd find it very strange that a lady was introduced onstage as the inspiration for a main character in that show."

"Why will that be so strange?"

"Because the show was a colossal flop. And because there is no way in hell that the main character of that show could have been based on a black hootchy-kootchy dancer. Not even one as elegant and world renowned as yourself."

"You mean they'll want to know who I really am?"

"Exactly. And why you're in Atlantic City. And why you're staying in the Monte Carlo. It just has to be checked out. Because that show is at the very center of the killings. Which brings me to . . . something else, Evie. Something else . . . concerning you . . . and the show."

She didn't ask what. She merely kept on driving . . . slow and steady.

Finally, when I could stand it no longer, I said, "Evie, don't you want to know what I was going to say next?"

"Why? It was something about being careful, wasn't it? You were going to tell me there's a chance they might try to do something bad to me."

"Yes. And that I'm going to protect you in every way I can. I doubt you're in real danger, but if anything were to happen—"

"I know. Like I said, I'm too old to waste time being scared. And besides, it wouldn't be the first time somebody's tried to send these old bones to their Maker. We've got to help that lady Carmella, or they'll send her to the chair."

"It's so wonderful of you to feel that way, Evie, when you don't even know Carmella."

"Well, neither do you. That's why I like you so much, young lady."

Then Evie burst into a chorus of "Every Honey."

An old hootchy-kootchy dancer is a force to be reckoned with.

We parked the rented car in the same underground garage where we had parked Art Agee's death car. Then we rode the elevator up to our floor.

Tony was waiting for us in the corridor . . . pacing . . . smoking. He was pale as a sheet.

The moment he saw me he grabbed my arm and began to talk.

"It was the strangest thing, Swede. Baretta and I are in your room, waiting. We hear someone enter the room next door. We hear them searching. Baretta busts through the door and I follow. Guess who's inside?"

"I don't know, Tony."

"Dressed in a casino janitor outfit."

"I don't know, Tony!"

"Carlos Weathers."

Chapter 16

Tony waited for an astonished response from me, but he was disappointed. I had no idea who Tony and Baretta would find in that room. No one would have shocked me. It was the process . . . the logic of the murders . . . that held my astonishment.

"What did he say when you caught him?"

"He denies anything and everything. He said he thought he was in your room. That he wanted to borrow your marked script of *Sweet Bird of Youth*. That he searched the apartment for it. When we asked why he was wearing a custodian outfit, he said that he had found it in a pail outside his room and that he'd always thought wearing the clothing of a stranger was the first step to understanding his character."

"Spare me! Is Harlow okay?"

"She's fine . . . in your room."

"Well, Tony, why don't you take Evie into my room and just wait there with her."

He took Evie by the arm and escorted her into the room. I waited until the door shut and then walked into the adjoining room.

It was a bizarre scene. Carlos Weathers in his janitor's jumpsuit seemed to be lounging on a sofa.

Detective Baretta was standing behind the sofa, casually staring out the window.

There was no sense of arrest . . . of crisis . . . of criminality.

I sat down at the far end of the sofa. Weathers stared at me.

"Who told you to come here?" I asked him.

He sat back and grinned harshly, but didn't answer.

I looked at Baretta. "Has he told you anything?"

"He shut up. He told me a cock-and-bull story about how he thought this was your room and then he shut up."

It was odd how the roles had been so dramatically reversed. Early in the morning he had berated me and led me in rehearsal like a child. And here we were again . . . but the scene was so different.

"He murdered them both," I said to Baretta, but continued staring at Carlos.

"What was he looking for here?" Baretta asked.

"Oh, nothing much this time. Just information. He was ordered to find out who that crazy old lady was who was called up to the bandstand in Surf World, claiming some kind of connection to a Broadway show called *Pie in Your Face*. But when he killed Adele Houghton he was looking for something really important . . . really concrete."

I pulled a photograph out of my purse and held it up to Weathers. He didn't flinch. He didn't speak. But he had stopped grinning.

Baretta walked over. "That isn't the photograph you showed me."

"No, it isn't. I showed you a torn photograph with only one young man—Ben Rios. The other man in the picture is Tobin Haggar."

He whistled in astonishment.

"Isn't this what you were looking for?" I asked Weathers, shoving it right under his nose. "Isn't this why you killed Adele? And Agee?"

He didn't say a word.

"I figured out everything, Mr. Weathers. The way I see it, you have only two options. Twenty years or the death penalty. This is New Jersey. Those are your options."

He didn't speak. He focused his eyes on the ceiling.

"What did you figure out?" Baretta asked angrily.

"Why Adele Houghton was murdered."

"Why don't you enlighten me."

"She was a compulsive gambler who won
. . . and won big. Won too much. The casinos
began to dislike her intensely, the way they
dislike and mistrust all chronic winners. Not
only did she win a lot of money but she was
extremely generous with her money. She lent
money to dealers and she lent money to a
young man who was very much in debt to
bookmakers. His name was Art Agee."

I looked at Carlos Weathers. He was silent.
His face was cast in bronze.

"Then, Detective Baretta, the casinos decided to ban Adele Houghton. If they couldn't
do it legally, they could make it uncomfort-
able for her. And they did. She couldn't gamble much anymore. She couldn't win. She
couldn't be generous.

"It was Art Agee who missed her gambling
most. He owed a lot of money. He decided
that Adele had to get back playing, but how to
persuade the casinos? He found a way. Somehow he obtained photos of a casino owner,
Tobin Haggar, and a mob figure. He knew
that if the Casino Gaming Commission knew
there was a longtime friendship between the
owner and the mobster, the owner would lose
his license.

"Art Agee gave the photos to Adele. She
used them as a form of blackmail to get back
into the casinos.

"And she got back in. And the money was

191

flowing again. But by then Tobin Haggar had decided to get the photos back no matter what it took. He wanted Adele off his back—at any cost. So he contacted his old friend Ben Rios, now in jail, and asked for help. Rios was owed many favors by many people."

I moved closer to Carlos Weathers. There was a pulse, a tick, on his brow. As though some miniature being just beneath the surface of his skin were fighting to push out. Weathers's eyes darted this way and that; anywhere but in my direction. He pretended not to be listening to the things I was saying to him, pretended that he was much too caught up in his own thoughts. He seemed to be composing some kind of stage instruction . . . moving actors around like salt shakers in his head. But no, I knew he was listening, and listening closely.

"One of the people who owed Rios a favor was a young man who had been in one of Rios's looted Broadway shows. He had helped Rios loot the production and he had been amply rewarded with enough money to start and maintain a theater in Chicago. Now the bill had come due."

It had all come out of my mouth so quickly and so surely that I had astonished even myself. I had constructed the whole cloth out of the bits and pieces that had come back to me. I had constructed it on a wing and a prayer.

Every single bit of it I could back up . . . every sentence I could support with the facts of the case if one could call such things facts. But I knew also that another person could have constructed an entirely different scenario based on the same facts.

I put my hand on Carlos Weathers's knee, as if I were a kindly, admiring aunt. "You killed them both, didn't you? You slashed poor Adele to death. And you shot Art Agee through the eye."

I watched him. I waited. Slowly, ever so slowly, I could see a change coming.

His face seemed to be crumbling a tiny section at a time.

A tear rolled down Carlos Weathers's face.

Then another. Then a flood. But he was still rigid. He had not collapsed.

He said in a startlingly calm voice: "I didn't mean to kill her. My job was to just get the photos back. That's all. I mean, yeah, I was supposed to hurt her some, but not to kill her. The thing was to scare her bad enough that she would never try blackmailing Tobin Haggar again.

"But I didn't figure on her being that tough. Even drunk, she fought like a tiger. When I burst into her room I was wearing a stocking over my face. I thought it would terrify her. But she seemed to think it was some kind of game. She thought it was one of her friends playing a joke on her. She told me to stick around because she was expecting one of her friends—Carmella—to come and join her any minute. Finally, she realized I wasn't kidding. She was even going to try to keep me there till she could call the police. I panicked. I cut her once and demanded the photos. She fought back wildly. She was crazy. Then finally, while we were struggling, she pulled the stocking off my face. Something inside of me just—well, I just kept slashing until she was dead. Until I'd . . . killed her. Then I ran before her friend arrived."

The tears stopped. He did a strange thing. He stretched out his arms, stiffly, and stared at his hands, as if to see whether or not they were shaking. They were not.

"And what was your reason for killing Art?" I asked. I could feel Detective Baretta behind me.

"I didn't kill him."

"Then who did?"

"Charlie Lott."

"Why?"

"I don't know."

"Was it because Charlie Lott and Tobin Haggar found out that it was Art who supplied the photos to Adele?"

"I don't know."

"Where is the knife you used on the woman?" Baretta asked.

Carlos pulled his hands back to his side. He smiled at Baretta, a very strange smile.

Then he catapulted himself out of the sofa and before our horrified eyes hurtled himself through the glass window.

What happened next is only a dim memory. I recall not doing a single thing at first . . . not speaking . . . not moving . . . not focusing on anything.

I recall that Baretta then started to curse . . . long and low and ugly . . . a stream of invective that seemed to propel him toward the shattered glass.

Then he sat down and picked up the telephone. He asked to be connected to 911.

Then I ran out of the room, screaming "Get help! Hurry, get help!" Help for whom?

Suddenly I was surrounded. People were pouring out of rooms and elevators. I saw Tony and Evie running toward me. I saw maids, security men, hotel guests, confused and half clothed.

Then I became very calm again. Gordon Seaver was standing in front of me.

"What is going on?" he asked, grabbing one of my hands.

"He jumped. He jumped out of the window!"

"Who did?"

"Carlos Weathers."

"What about the show?"

One short, powerfully loud hoot of laughter escaped from my throat then. I wondered if I looked as stupid as I felt.

People continued to run past us. I began to hear sirens. I could see the back of Tony's head in the room I had vacated. He was staring at the smashed window.

"Everything will be fine, Gordon. Trust me."

"No it won't. Not without a director. I need a director."

We had lapsed into a kind of thespian psychosis.

"We'll do Shakespeare," I said.

"I can't do Shakespeare," he said.

"Oh yes you can, Gordon. Listen. Repeat after me. 'If this be error . . .' "

" 'If this be error . . .' "

" 'And upon me proved . . .' "

" 'And upon me proved . . .' "

" 'I never writ . . .' "

" 'I never writ . . .' "

" 'And no man ever loved.' "

" 'And no man ever loved.' "

"You see, Gordon, you are a wonderful Shakespearean actor."

And then I started to weep and pushed his stupid hand away.

Chapter 17

I wish I could say that justice was served before I left Atlantic City. But it wasn't. Baretta did find a bloody stocking in Carlos Weathers's room, which confirmed that Weathers had indeed murdered Adele. But, with Weathers dead, there was nothing to tie Charlie Lott and Tobin Haggar to Adele's murder, and specially to Art's murder. Weathers's confession had neither been recorded nor signed before he made what was certainly a more impressive exit than I'd ever seen any actor pull off.

Detective Baretta assured me, however, that the photos would be delivered to the New Jersey Gaming Commission and it was highly probable that Tobin Haggar and Charlie Lott would be asked to leave Atlantic City and never come back.

I also wish I could say the remaining mysteries surrounding young Art Agee were cleared up. But they weren't. Did Agee really have a short affair with Carmella? Or had he only told me that as a ploy? Had his affair in fact been with Adele?

And why had me asked me to investigate? Did he want me to find the photos because he knew that Tobin Haggar found out that he'd given them to Adele? Had Tobin Haggar threatened him—threatened to kill him—if the photographs weren't returned? Or was Art simply going to pick up the blackmailing of Haggar where Adele left off, using another partner perhaps?

Nor can I say that the Valentine's Day performance was a success, even in its truncated form. We agreed—Gordon and I—that the only logical thing was to do the sonnets of Shakespeare . . . love poems extraordinaire . . . although, of course, scholars are unable to decide whether they were written to a young woman or a young man. We read from open books, seated on stools. We were mildly applauded. At the end, Gordon threw caution to the wind and recited a very maudlin Robert Burns love song, and then, after receiving a very ecstatic reception from an increasingly tipsy audience, launched into a medley of songs from *Finian's Rainbow*.

As for the voodoo cat, the lovely Harlow, aka Miss Otis, and as for my good friend Evie Soames . . . well, there was a less than unqualified happy ending there, too.

I gave Harlow to Evie. Both obviously needed a home and a friend. Evie, I reasoned, could keep on gambling and, with Harlow, keep on winning.

I didn't hear from Evie for at least two weeks after I came back to Manhattan.

It was a dreary day and I had been out shopping. When I returned, I picked up the mail, walked up the stairs, and found a very disgruntled Tony in my loft. He was broke, he said, and he wanted a drink and a good meal, and he blamed me for giving the voodoo cat to Evie because he needed the money more than she and he could have made a fortune gambling and he could have taken me to Paris and Istanbul and Milan . . . on and on he went.

Of course I had grown used to it so I let him babble. I looked through the mail. There was a letter from Evie. I sat down at the table and read it.

"Dear Alice:
I want to thank you for everything. Particularly Harlow. She is a very kind and loving friend. We spend a lot of time together. I must tell you a sad story, though. I rubbed Harlow's back eleven times and went to Atlantic City yesterday. I lost all the money you gave me. Do

you think Harlow's voodoo only works before Valentine's Day?
Love, Evie
The Oldest Living Hootchy-Kootchy Dancer in the Mid-Atlantic States."

I was about to give the letter to Tony. But then, I thought, No. He's better angry than depressed. I grabbed Bushy in my arms, blew a kiss to Pancho, sat back, and listened to the gambler's lament.

When he was finished, Bushy and I were half asleep at the table.

Suddenly he grabbed Bushy out of my arms. "I'm going to stroke Bushy twenty-six times . . . turn him into a voodoo cat and win eleven million dollars at the dice tables."

"You'd better be careful. Bushy might stroke you back."

"You're right!" He dropped Bushy onto the floor.

"Actually, I'd rather stroke you," he said.

"It's a bit early in the day, Tony."

He smiled. "You know, Swede, you were damn brilliant in Atlantic City."

"I don't think I was brilliant. Not really. Things just fell into place."

"It all makes sense now. After the fact. Doesn't it?"

"A lot of it. For example, the only two

major players in the case were absent when Adele was murdered."

"You mean they claim to have been absent."

"Right. Charlie Lott was supposed to be on vacation. And Carlos Weathers was delayed en route. So they said. But they were really there. Isn't that always the case, Tony? Smart criminals think of alibis. Who could suspect them? They weren't there."

"What I don't understand is your switch."

"Switch? What do you mean?"

"Well, you kept on harping that Adele was murdered to get the cat. Then, suddenly, you changed gears."

"After I saw the photographs . . . after I found out who those two young men were. Then I changed gears. I was logical. Suddenly, the idea of a voodoo cat seemed absurd. I realized it didn't matter why or how Adele was winning. The casinos wanted her out of their playing area. But it was Evie who told me that casinos ban chronic winners. That would never even dawn on me. Never."

"But how did you make the connection between the Broadway show and the murder? I admit your putting Evie up on the stage to flush out the killer was inspired . . . and a bit mad, like all inspirations. But how did you get from point A to point B? Was it a lucky guess?"

"Not really. It was because of that stupid

song. Art Agee told me that Adele sang it for Carmella on the night of the murder. It meant nothing to me at all until you told me about how Ben Rios had looted the show in which the song was performed. Too much of a coincidence, Tony, too much."

"Did you really think that trap would flush out a killer?"

"All I knew was, if the conspiracy had to do with that show and I were part of the conspiracy, I'd be most interested in a dotty old black lady claiming to be the inspiration for a leading role in that show. I'd want to know why she knows an obscure song from that deservedly obscure show. And why has she suddenly shown up in Atlantic City? Who is she? And isn't it interesting that she's staying in Tobin Haggar's casino? Yes, I'd have to check her out fast."

"Of course, there would have been an easier way to solve the whole case."

"What do you mean?"

"Get one of the old Playbills. Find out who was in *Pie in Your Face,* then just check the cast against all the suspects."

I was impressed. "You know, Tony, that never occurred to me. But it would just be anecdotal evidence." I laughed.

"What's so funny?"

"I have a feeling that Tobin's right-hand man . . ."

"You mean the head of security?"

"Right. Charlie Lott. I have the feeling that he was in that show."

"Why do you say that?"

"He's a chubby, out-of-shape, middle-aged man, but I saw him catch a falling container of coffee in midflight. He moved with the grace and quickness of an old song-and-dance man."

"A song-and-dance man . . . a hootchy-kootchy dancer . . . a bizarre stage director . . . what else is missing, Swede?"

"The real Adele Houghton," I replied sadly.

"She was one weird lady."

"I would like to have known her . . . to have tried to understand why she constructed that strange double life."

"Even labor lawyers can get bitten by compulsive gambling."

"But she gave a lot of her money away. And she constantly flirted with exposure. It was reckless of her to persuade her friends to have their annual reunion in Atlantic City— just asking for trouble. She must have had some reason for it. But I'll never know what it was."

"You know, Swede, it is possible that many men loved her."

"What a strange thing to say, Tony."

"I don't think so. A lot of men like wild women. I sure do."

"She would have been too much for you, Tony."

"You're too much for me."

"What a nice thing to say."

"Swede?"

"Yes, Tony."

"Will you marry me, Swede?"

"No."

"Then how about making me a grilled cheese sandwich?"

"Now that is wild, Tony!"

**Preview the next
adventure of**

**Alice Nestleton,
cat-sitter extraordinaire . . .**

A Cat in Fine Style

Preview the next
adventure of

Alice Nestleton,
cat-sitter extraordinaire . . .

A Cat in Fine Style

Chapter 1

"This is nuts," Basillio said, rubbing his hands together. "I don't know why *I'm* getting so nervous. I'm not the one doing this stupid thing."

"Maybe Tony's right, Aunt Alice. I feel very foolish."

The paint-flecked doors of the rickety old elevator slammed shut behind us.

So, both my niece and my friend Tony Basillio thought this venture was silly. What could I say? It wasn't easy to think of a defense for it.

Alison and I were going to be part of a fashion spread, odd as that sounds. There was a theme to the layout: different generations of photogenic women modeling original fashions by two trendy downtown *couturieres*. There would be mothers and daughters in matching ball gowns, grandmothers and granddaughters in silk baseball jackets. That sort of thing.

And then there would be Alison and me—

wearing identical scanty camisoles. It was all part of the lingerie-as-daywear craze.

Foolish? Well, I suppose I did feel a little foolish. But we were being offered unbelievably good pay for a couple of days' work, and I'd been through the torture of losing twelve pounds for the camera. So I wasn't about to get back on that infernal elevator and go home.

Grace Ann and Samantha Collins, the two fashion designer sisters who had recently hit it big in the fashion world, had once been my cat-sitting clients. They had operated a little boutique in Chelsea for years, selling their hand-loomed woolens and exquisite silk scarves and impeccably tailored working women's skirts to a very loyal and very discriminating clientele, but a limited one. I myself treasure the one and only Collins-made item I've ever owned: a long velvet skirt of midnight blue, which I received as a Christmas gift one year from a friend whose husband's death had left her with more money than sense, and to whom the act of shopping had become life itself.

The talented Collins sisters went on for years just managing to make ends meet—just. And then, for whatever reason, or possibly for no reason whatever, Boutique Ariel (so named because Ariel had been their mother's name) and the two sisters behind it caught fire. In the past year or so, they'd designed the wedding gowns of more than two dozen high-profile New York brides. They were being featured in all the "important" industry publications and their clothing was turning up at A-list gatherings at A-list restaurants on the backs of A-list celebrities.

Now, what in God's name did this world of society brides and gossip columns and *Harper's Bazaar* spreads have to do with me? Nothing. Absolutely nothing. So when Grace Ann Collins phoned me one day about a month ago, I assumed she needed me to look after Bobbin, the big blue point Himalayan cat I'd had so much fun with a couple of years ago while the sisters were on a buying trip in Savannah.

But no. What Grace Ann wanted was to photograph me! She and Samantha were promoting an extensive line of underwear-inspired fashions that were all the rage among the trend-conscious young—and the not so young.

"As far as fashion goes, Alice," she had said, "you are well nigh hopeless. It's your milky white skin that interests us. And your torso. And your marvelous long legs of course. I just know you're going to be fabulous in those airy little things of ours. And really, honey, what woman wouldn't want to be shot by Fliss?"

Fliss? What was that—a bug spray?

"Fliss Francis! Fliss Francis!" had been her incredulous reply. Did I mean to say I'd never heard of the award-winning British photographer? The one who was going to immortalize me, Grace Ann promised.

Alice Nestleton, fashion model. It was absurd, obviously, and I was on the verge of telling her so. But then she named a ballpark figure for the fee I'd receive for the assignment. I said I'd think it over.

Grace Ann phoned me again three days later. She and Samantha had their hearts set on having me as a model, torso and all. And the price had gone up. Before the conversation was over, I'd given her my niece's phone number as well. Alison, at least, had heard of Fliss Francis.

And that is how we came to be in this lovingly renovated cast iron building on Greene Street—well, everything but the nerve-rattling elevator had been renovated. Today's photo session was taking place in a glamorous Soho loft belonging to someone named Niles Wiegel, who, to the best of my knowledge, was neither artist nor photographer nor designer nor Indian chief. He was simply someone with money whom other people with money knew. That sort of thing isn't exclusive to Soho, I guess, but it surely seemed that way.

The door to the loft apartment swung open to reveal a hive of activity. In fact, the scene was not unlike the backstage atmosphere in a theater a few days before opening. There were lights and flats and wardrobe racks and cartons stacked or stashed or flung here and there. Half a dozen people moved frantically about the apartment, to no apparent purpose.

I spotted Samantha Collins, knee deep in chiffon, peering critically at a spaghetti-strap nightgown on a puffy satin hanger.

Samantha and Grace Ann were both lovely, smart women. Both in their early fifties, both looking younger than that, both reed-thin. Both dyed-in-the-wool New Yorkers born in Mississippi and raised in genteel poverty by an ambitious iron butterfly of a mother from one of those mythic "good" southern families.

But where Grace Ann was independent, garrulous, and shrewd—a kind of modern-day belle—her sister Samantha worked more behind the scenes. She did a great deal of the seamstressing work and took her pleasure not in lunching with fashion magazine editors but in tending the impressive garden behind the first-floor apartment of the brownstone the two had shared for some twenty-five years.

"Alice, Alice, Alice!" I heard my name repeated in a barely perceptible Southern drawl.

Grace Ann, in a perfect black knit jumper, white shirt, and antique high-button boots, came floating toward us. She kissed me lightly on each cheek, then bestowed the same blessing on Alison.

"Grace Ann," I said, "this is my . . . this is Tony Basillio."

"My, aren't you handsome?" she said immediately.

Tony cleared his throat and took her hand.

"I hope it's all right that I brought Tony along. He was inordinately curious and I didn't think anyone would mind."

"Of course not. We can always make use of a strong back."

Alison smirked, relishing the dig.

"Fliss isn't here yet," Grace Ann said. "I can't abide tardiness, can you? Except in a genius, of course. Come along now and meet the others."

Samantha had noticed us by then and waved distractedly in our direction.

A thin man dressed all in black cashmere, about thirty-five years old, flew through the room then, calling his hellos over one shoulder. He was carrying a pitcher of tomato juice.

"That was Niles," Grace Ann pronounced. "He and Lainie were good enough to let us invade their home for the day. Which brings me to—"

Grace Ann broke off then and turned to grasp the hand of the tall man in impeccably fitted jeans who had walked up behind her.

"—which brings me to my lovely Hector. Hector Naciemento. He and Niles are old friends."

It was obvious from the way she interlaced her fingers with his and looked up into his liquid eyes that the two of them were more than "lovely" friends. Well well well—as my grandmother used to say when something juicy was told to her—so Grace Ann had a young lover.

Hector was a sublimely beautiful man with huge, transporting eyes the color of espresso and flawless, tanned skin. The pushed-up sleeves of his white sweatshirt set off the muscles in his upper arms like sapphires around the star diamond in a lady's brooch. Alison turned on a 14-karat smile as he caressed her hand in greeting. Tony seemed almost embarrassed, looking down at the floor as he shook hands. Hector murmured something to me about having been told how lovely I was, but, frankly, I wasn't really listening. There was something almost hypnotic about his good looks.

"And this is Penny," I heard Grace Ann say. "She'll be helping with your makeup."

Penny Motion might have been as attractive an exemplar of young female beauty as

Hector was of masculine good looks. But the picture she presented undercut that severely. Her skin was powdered to give the effect of library paste, her wonderful light green eyes seemed buried in the crudely drawn black circles beneath them, and her lipstick was a ghastly purplish black. Her jeans were more tatters than fabric, and on her feet were laceless combat boots that looked as if they'd seen active duty in at least two long wars.

Penny nodded curtly at the three of us and plopped a heavy case into Hector's arms. He smiled indulgently at her and then followed her over to a desk in the corner of the room.

"Can I get anyone a Bloody Mary?"

The speaker was a pleasant-looking woman, barely thirty years old, I'd say, also dressed in severe Soho black, with auburn hair pulled back into a ponytail.

"Hi, I'm Lainie Wiegel," she said. "Exciting, isn't it? Is everybody stoked for Fliss?"

Before I could answer, Samantha Collins stepped up and took my arm. "All right, Alice, Alison, let's see what we have here."

That was her way of saying it was time for us to change. She took a ruffled bed jacket and held it up to Alison's face as if assessing the appropriateness of the color for my niece.

Tony alone accepted Lainie's offer of a drink. I watched them disappear into the kitchen area.

Samantha busied herself undoing the zipper of my drab corduroy dress. "Well, dear," she said, "let's have a look at you. Hmmm. Haven't you lost just pounds and pounds of weight? . . . Oh . . . No, you haven't."

I laughed in spite of the insult. "I did my best, Samantha."

"I'm sure you'll be just fine. At least you know how to walk and how to stand still. You're an actress. Oh, Alice, you know Sidney, don't you?"

Standing in my slip, I looked over at the late-middle-age man in wire-rim glasses who was handing Samantha a scissor. "No," I said simply.

"No? I was sure you'd met. Well, Alice, this is our attorney, Sidney Rickover. Sidney, this is Alice Nestleton."

"A pleasure," Mr. Rickover said and quickly backed away from my seminakedness. I noticed how carefully he lifted his feet and set them down again, as if afraid to make a noise. Where had Sidney come from? He had to have been in the loft all along, but I had never even noticed him.

"And this is Alison Chevigny," Samantha added. "Isn't she adorable?"

Sidney Rickover's smile indicated that if Samantha thought she was, then he thought she was.

"Samantha, I think that covers just about

everything," he said. "If you'll sign all three copies of those papers—"

"Yes, Sidney, we'll get to it today, I promise."

Mr. Rickover leaned forward slightly as if to kiss Samantha's cheek, but at that very moment she turned back to me.

"Goodbye, Sidney," she said.

"Oh no, Sidney! You mustn't leave yet." That was Grace Ann, who had joined us. "You must go over that lease, Sidney. I've got half a dozen questions you simply must answer before I can even *think* about signing."

"Of course, Grace Ann."

With that, the two of them walked off.

From time to time Basillio popped up here and there in the loft. I heard Niles explaining to him how the computer worked. A few minutes later I spotted Basillio toting lighting equipment under the supervision of Penny Motion, who barked out directions as they made their way across the floor. Then I thought I heard him lecturing Lainie on the proper way to steam milk for cappuccino. Only once did I catch him peering behind the screen and into the makeshift dressing room that Samantha had set up for Alison and me.

This was like a rehearsal that had no payoff. No opening night, no performance. Just an endless rehearsal. I was growing tired of Samantha's ministrations and impatient with

Penny's ongoing application of paint to my face. It was especially disturbing that I couldn't see what she was doing to me. I kept thinking that perhaps she wanted to make me over in her own spooky image.

I saw Alison regarding herself in the free-standing full length mirror. She looked part waif and part sex kitten in her pink camisole. There was an expression on her face I couldn't quite decipher. Was she pleased with herself or was she appalled at what she'd gotten herself into?

What *I'd* gotten her into—that was the truth of it. As the day wore on, I became increasingly ashamed of having involved her in this ridiculous enterprise. I wondered if Felix, my nieces's older and very paternal lover, would hold this against me forever.

The heady aroma of Italian roast coffee filled the loft. I changed into a robe and went to get a cup. After I'd had my little break, I went off in search of the bathroom.

Lord, I got a terrible scare when I pulled open the sliding door to the bedroom at the rear of the loft!

It was as if a fur coat had come to life and was preparing to ravage me.

Jumping from the high loft bed, straight at me, was Bobbin! Humongous blue Bobbin, who seemed to be the size of a pony.

"God, Bobbin! You scared the daylights out of me."

The big ball of fur rubbed against my ankles. I leaned down and roughed him up a bit.

"That's right, you old bear. It's me, Alice. What are you doing in this place?"

Bobbin seemed to bristle at the question. He drew himself up haughtily and retreated behind the armoire.

When I rejoined the group, Niles and Lainie were winding their way around the room, offering trays of sandwiches and snacks to the others. Tony came bounding up to me.

"Swede, I have to admit I thought this was going to be another one of your debacles. But it's great!"

"Oh, you think so, do you, Tony?"

"Yeah. I mean," he dropped his voice a little then, "I thought these people were going to be downtown pinheads—too much money and no aesthetics. But they're nice. Except for that weird-looking girl, I mean. But she's kind of interesting, too. Kind of subverbal. Lainie was a theater major at Bennington, did you know that? And listen, how come you don't wear things like that all the time?" He pointed to the sheer spaghetti strap gown Samantha had been examining earlier.

"Probably for the same reason you don't wear things like that all the time, Tony."

"Come on, loosen up, Swede. I think it's

going pretty well. Let me get you a sandwich. That guy Niles just made his special pâté in that . . . that thing . . . that blender thing."

"No sandwiches for me. I don't want to get one of those looks from Samantha. I just want that photographer to get here so I can put this all behind me."

Samantha helped Alison and me into matching plain white muslin slips, then ice blue bias-cut nightgowns, then yellow boxer shorts.

Penny Motion was good at her job. She made us look like Times Square hookers and then, with the help of a couple of old-fashioned hair rollers, like sex-starved trailer park housewives; she even made us up to look as though we were wearing no makeup at all.

And still Fliss Francis, the tardy genius, did not arrive. At one o'clock I broke down and went into the kitchen looking for leftover pâté.

Niles Wiegel was seated on a kitchen stool in front of, as Tony had called it, that blender thing. He was whipping up another one of his specialities, no doubt.

"I was wondering," I said, "if there's anything left to eat. I don't care about my cheekbones anymore."

Niles said nothing. In fact, there was no sign he'd heard me come in.

I spoke more loudly this time. "Excuse me, Niles."

He remained perfectly still. His profile was oddly cast.

I walked over to the counter. Niles's right hand was resting on the control panel of the Cuisinart. I tapped him once on the shoulder and he slid easily off his seat, like fine Chinese silk, not stopping until he hit the tiled floor. Very hard.

Oh my. I stepped back, suddenly cold.

"I think you'd better come in here," I called into the other room.

"Who?" Grace Ann answered back.

"All of you."

I heard Lainie Wiegel scream.

Tony sighed heavily. And I think he uttered a curse.

Hector Naciemento and Sidney Rickover rushed over to the motionless body.

Sidney reached down into Niles's black T-shirt, groping for a pulse at the side of his neck.

"He's . . . There's no . . . He's dead," the attorney said.

Lainie cried out again and fell into Grace Ann's arms.

Samantha covered her mouth with both hands.

"What shall we do?" asked Hector softly.

"Call somebody?" Penny suggested.

I felt Alison's fingers around my wrist. She was hurting me. I gently guided her backward, into Tony's hold.

Just then there was a commotion at the front door. "Hello! Hey, Niles? Anyone home?"

Fliss Francis had arrived at last.

ENTER THE
MYSTERIOUS WORLD OF
ALICE NESTLETON IN
HER LYDIA ADAMSON
SERIES . . . BY READING
THESE OTHER PURR-FECT
CAT CAPERS FROM SIGNET

A CAT IN THE MANGER

Alice Nestleton, an off-off Broadway actress-turned-amateur sleuth, is crazy about cats, particularly her Maine coon Bushy and alleycat Pancho. Alice plans to enjoy a merry little Christmas peacefully cat-sitting at a gorgeous Long Island estate where she expects to be greeted by eight howling Himalayans. Instead, she stumbles across a grisly corpse. Alice has unwittingly become part of a deadly game of high-sakes horse racing, sinister seduction, and missing money. Alice knows she'll have to count on her catlike instincts and (she hopes!) nine lives to solve the murder mystery.

A CAT OF A DIFFERENT COLOR

Alice Nestleton returns home one evening after teaching her acting class at the New School to find a lovestruck student bearing a curious gift—a beautiful white Abyssinianlike cat. The next day, the student is murdered in a Manhattan bar and the rare cat is catnapped! Alice's feline curiosity prompts her to investigate. As the clues unfold, Alice is led into an underworld of smuggling, blackmail, and murder. Alice sets one of her famous traps to uncover a criminal operation that stretches from downtown Manhattan to South America to the center of New York's diamond district. Alice herself becomes the prey in a cat-and-mouse game before she finds the key to the mystery in a group of unusual cats with an exotic history.

A CAT IN WOLF'S CLOTHING

When two retired city workers are found slain in their apartment, the New York City police discover the same clue that has left them baffled in 17 murder cases in the last 15 years—all of the murder victims were cat owners, and a toy was left for each cat at the murder scene. After reaching one too many dead ends, the police decide to consult New York's cagiest crime-solving cat expert, Alice Nestleton. What appears to be the work of one psychotic, cat-loving murderer leads to a tangled web of intrigue as our heroine becomes convinced that the key to the crimes lies in the cats, which mysteriously vanish after the murders. The trail of clues takes Alice from the secretive small towns of the Adirondacks to the eerie caverns beneath Central Park, where she finds that sometimes cat-worship can lead to murder.

A CAT BY ANY OTHER NAME

A hot New York summer has Alice Nestleton taking a hiatus from the stage and joining a coterie of cat-lovers in cultivating a Manhattan herb garden. When one of the cozy group plunges to her death, Alice is stunned and grief-stricken by the apparent suicide of her close friend. But aided by her two cats, she soon smells a rat. And with the help of her own felinelike instincts, Alice unravels the trail of clues and sets a trap that leads her from the Brooklyn Botanic Gardens right to her own backyard. Could the victim's dearest friends have been her own worst enemies?

A CAT IN THE WINGS

Cats, Christmas, and crime converge when Alice Nestleton finds herself on the prowl for the murderer of a once-world-famous ballet dancer. Alice's close friend has been charged with the crime and it is up to Alice to seek the truth. From Manhattan's meanest streets to the elegant salons of wealthy art patrons, Alice is drawn into a dark and dangerous web of deception, until one very special cat brings Alice the clues she needs to track down the murderer of one of the most imaginative men the ballet world has ever known.

A CAT WITH A FIDDLE

Alice Nestleton's latest job requires her to drive a musician's cat up to rural Massachusetts. The actress, hurt by bad reviews of her latest play, looks forward to a long, restful weekend. But though the woods are beautiful and relaxing, Alice must share the artists' colony with a world-famous quartet beset by rivalries. Her peaceful vacation is shattered when the handsome ladykiller of a pianist turns up murdered. Alice may have a tin ear, but she also has a sharp eye for suspects and a nose for clues. Her investigations lead her from the scenic Berkshire mountains to New York City, but it takes the clue of a rare breed of cats for Alice to piece together the puzzle. Alice has a good idea whodunit, but the local police won't listen, so our intrepid cat-lady is soon baiting a dangerous trap for a killer.

A CAT IN A GLASS HOUSE

Alice Nestleton, after years off-off Broad-way, sees stardom on the horizon at last. Her agent has sent her to a chic Tribeca Chinese restaurant to land a movie part with an up-and-coming film producer. Instead, Alice finds herself right in the middle of cats, crime, and mayhem once again. Before she can place her order, she sees a beautiful red tabby mysteriously perched amid the glass decor of the restaurant . . . and three young thugs pulling out weapons to spray the restaurant with bullets. A waitress is killed, and Alice is certain the cat is missing, too. Teamed up with a handsome, Mandarin-speaking cop, Alice is convinced the missing cat and the murder are related, and she sets out to prove it.

A CAT WITH NO REGRETS

Alice Nestleton is on her way to stardom! Seated aboard a private jet en route to Marseilles, with her cats Bushy and Pancho beside her, she eagerly anticipates her first starring role in a feature film. To her further delight, the producer, Dorothy Dodd, has brought her three beautiful Abyssinian cats along. But on arrival in France, tragedy strikes. Before Alice's horrified eyes, the van driven by Dorothy Dodd goes out of control and crashes, killing the producer immediately. As the cast and crew scramble to keep their film project alive, Alice has an additional worry: what will happen to Dorothy's cats? As additional corpses turn up to mar the beautiful Provençal countryside, Alice becomes convinced the suspicious deaths and the valuable cats are related. She sets one of her famous traps to solve the mystery.

A CAT ON THE CUTTING EDGE

What do you do if your beloved kitty
suddenly becomes a snarling, hissing
tiger when you try to coax him into his
carrier for a routine trip to the vet? If
you're savvy, cat-sitting sleuth Alice
Nestleton, you call for help from the Village Cat People, a service for cat owners with problem pets. Yet Pancho's
unruliness becomes the least of Alice's
worries when her Cat People representa-
tive, Martha, is found murdered at
Alice's front door. Martha's friends
sense foul play and ask Alice to investigate. Alice would much rather focus her
attention on her new loft apartment in
twisty, historic Greenwich Village. But a
second murder involving the Cat People
gives her "paws." When a series of clues
leads Alice to a Bohemian poet and
trendy New York's colorful past, the Village becomes the perfect place to catch
a killer.

Lydia Adamson is the pseudonym
of a noted mystery writer
who lives in New York.

Alice Nestleton fans who share her love for four-legged friends will purr over the Dr. Deirdre Quinn Nightingale series.

DR. NIGHTINGALE
RIDES THE ELEPHANT

A country vet gets a circus for a client . . . and an animal act that's a real killer.

DR. NIGHTINGALE COMES HOME

When a spunky veterinarian investigates all creatures great and small . . . to find a two-legged killer.

DR. NIGHTINGALE GOES
TO THE DOGS

When a spunky vet sniffs into murder, a monastery famous for its German shepherds becomes a real animal house.

Available from Signet

MYSTERY FAVORITES

MYSTERY ANTHOLOGIES

☐ **MURDER ON TRIAL** *13 Courtroom Mysteries By the Masters of Detection.* Attorney and clients, judges and prosecutors, witnesses and victims all meet in this perfect locale for outstanding mystery fiction. Now, subpoenaed from the pages of *Alfred Hitchcock's Mystery Magazine* and *Ellery Queen Mystery Magazine*—with the sole motive of entertaining you—are tales brimming with courtroom drama.

(177215—$4.99)

☐ **ROYAL CRIMES, New Tales of Blue-Bloody Murder,** by Robert Barnard, Sharyn McCrumb, H. R. F. Keating, Peter Lovesey, Edward Hoch and 10 others. Edited by Maxim Jakubowski and Martin H. Greenberg. From necromancy in the reign of Richard II to amorous pussyfooting by recent prime ministers, heavy indeed is the head that wears the crown, especially when trying to figure out whodunit ... in fifteen brand new stories of murder most royal. (181115—$4.99)

☐ **MURDER FOR MOTHER** by Ruth Rendell, Barbara Collins, Billie Sue Mosiman, Bill Crider, J. Madison Davis, Wendy Hornsby, and twelve more. These eighteen works of short fiction celebrate Mother's Day with a gift of great entertainment ... a story collection that every mystery-loving mama won't want to miss.

(180364—$4.99)

☐ **MURDER FOR FATHER** 20 Mystery Stories by Ruth Rendell, Ed Gorman, Barbara Collins, and 7 More Contemporary Writers of Detective Fiction. Here are proud papas committing crimes, solving cases, or being role models for dark deeds of retribution, revenge, and of course, murder. (180682—$4.99)

*Prices slightly higher in Canada

Buy them at your local bookstore or use this convenient coupon for ordering.

PENGUIN USA
P.O. Box 999 — Dept. #17109
Bergenfield, New Jersey 07621

Please send me the books I have checked above.
I am enclosing $_____ (please add $2.00 to cover postage and handling). Send check or money order (no cash or C.O.D.'s) or charge by Mastercard or VISA (with a $15.00 minimum). Prices and numbers are subject to change without notice.

Card #_____ Exp. Date _____
Signature_____
Name_____
Address_____
City _____ State _____ Zip Code _____

For faster service when ordering by credit card call **1-800-253-6476**

Allow a minimum of 4-6 weeks for delivery. This offer is subject to change without notice.